My husband and I are both in the B.D.S.M., community own sissy maid slave who week on average to help us keep the house clean. Isabel our maid works on a reward scheme, if she is good and works hard she gets treats and if she is bad she gets punished usually with a cane or strap.

Although we are both very much part of the B.D.S.M., community our lives changed completely when one summer we were on holiday in Kent. We both have a passion for visiting stately homes and manor houses. We loved to see how the other half lives and we enjoyed walking in well-manicured lawns and gardens. We had just finished visiting a stately home and were on our way back to our hotel tired after a long but enjoyable day in the hot sunshine. It was a lovely afternoon and we had travelled about ten miles from the stately home back towards our hotel when my husband Bert, who was driving, swerved to avoid some glass in the road, but he was too late in the manoeuvre and punctured a tyre on the back of the car.

Bert flew into a rage and spent several minutes indulging himself in the tide of expletives whic included throwing his hands in the air and shaking the steering wheel in temper. Then when recovered from his tantrums he decided to change the tyre. It was a hot stifling day so I go out of the car too. Bert refused my help, although there was nothing I could actually do to help, changing a tyre was a one-man job. So decided to fetch my bottle of water and go for a short stroll leaving Bert to it. I ambled up the narrow county road admiring the meadows and mature beach trees when I saw in the distance a big house as we had an interest in big houses it took my attention and I decided to take a closer look.

I knew Bert couldn't go anywhere without me, so he would just have to wait until I returned once he had fixed the tyre. The big house was a couple of fields away, and as I didn't know how to get to it by road, I decided to go across the meadow to take a closer look. I walked for about fifteen minutes across a field and I could see the grand house it was abandoned and empty. It was a beautiful house in a French Chateaux style. I could see some of the tiles and slates had come off the roof and an odd smashed window. I was distracted by a horn blasting behind me and realised Bert had driven up the road to find me. I decided to leave what I was doing and go back to Bert and the car before he throws another tantrum.

On reaching the car I jumped in and embraced the cool of the car's air conditioner as it was a blazingly hot day. As I recovered from the heat Bert said:

"I have been waiting for ages for you," he remonstrated with some annoyance in his voice. but he gave me a peck on the cheek, all the same, to demonstrate he is isn't that angry with me. "Why were you in the middle of that field, what had you seen?" He asked.

"There's an old dilapidated house, you can just make it out if you look," I said, pointing in the direction of the neglected house.

"I see it, what of it?" Bert asked.

"I want you to find it for me by road for me, I want to take a closer look," I said in my most endearing and pleading voice.

"Bridget, it's getting late, we should be thinking about dinner, not going on wild goose chases. I have no idea where to go to find the house or where to start looking."

'If we drive around enough, we'll find it," I assured Bert.

"You have half an hour, if we can't find the house in half an hour, I'm finding a decent pub for dinner my tummy is already beginning to rumble."

"Okay a deal, come on, let's go," I said enthusiastically. We drive around and around and just as Bert was about to give up, we discovered a wide gravel drive with a broken gate and concrete pillars.

"This leads somewhere, it could be the drive to the house I was looking at, let's take a look.

"It could be anyone's drive," Bert insisted, "we'll be trespassing."

"I doubt it, look at the state of the gate, it's falling to pieces. If we are in somebody's drive, we can just turn around and drive out, don't be such a fuss pot. Come on, let's look I am sure it belongs to the house I saw." I assured Bert.

Bert crunched the car into gear and we lurched forward and drove cautiously down the gravel drive. It was a long and winding drive and eventually, we came out in a clearing and stood before us was a dilapidated manor house. The beautiful house looked forlorn and neglected, nevertheless, it still oozed character and charm. We left the car to take a closer look at the building. Bert just saw the house as a ruin, but I could see the potential and it deserved to be brought back to its former glory.

"I want it," I said aloud.

"Don't be daft, it may be in a ruinous state, but it is still worth a fortune and what do we use for money to repair it, buttons, or seashells? Not to mention the staff needed to maintain a house this size and heating and electric costs, Bridget, ou're in cloud cuckoo land," Bert said dismissing the whole idea.

I wonder if we can peek inside," I mused. I walked up to the front door which was rotten and although locked was easy to push open. We stepped inside to immediately see a beautiful grand staircase. Okay, it was all rotten and falling to bits, but I could imagine myself in an evening frock sliding down those stairs to greet my guests. However, I had to concede Bert was right, how could we afford it and run such a house, even if we could buy it?

Okay," I said, returning to reality, "let's go and have dinner." We climbed back into the car and drove until we spotted a nice country pub. It was a lovely pub with oak beams and an old worldly feel to it. We both had sea bass and sweet potatoes and green beans.

"Any idea about where we are going to visit tomorrow," Bert asked as he finished his meal and sat back ready to enjoy a glass of whiskey.

"Over near the entrance where we came in is a rack of pamphlets I will go and get a selection may give us an idea of how to amuse ourselves tomorrow," I said, jumping up and returning with an ample handful of leaflets and passed half to Bert and I read the reminder.

"There is Frobisher Hall, which is open to the public and it isn't too far away from our hotel,' Bert advised me, "we could go and take a look. It might be worth a visit."

"Look what I have found," I said interpreting Bert, "this is a booklet of properties for sale and guess what?" I added excitedly.

"What?" Bert asked.

"Windrush Manor is for sale," I said, showing Bert the entry in the magazine.

"What is special about Windrush Manor?" Bert asked, glancing at the booklet.

"Don't you recognise it?" I asked.

"Nope," Bert replied.

"It's the derelict house we were looking at this afternoon. I know the picture shows it in better days, but it is the same house I am sure," I said enthusiastically.

"How much is it?" Bert asked.

"I don't know, it says P.O.A., I think that means the price is on an application or something similar. Can we go to the estate agents tomorrow and inquire about it, please?"

"No," Bert said decisively, " why get yourself in a state over something you know you can't have?" Bert decided for me there is no way we could afford it. I knew if I made enough fuss and pleaded long enough Bert, being the softy he is, deep down, will change his mind.

"Go on," I pleaded, "Pretty Please. I will love you forever and ever. It wouldn't hurt just to speak to the agent."

"I don't suppose it would hurt just to inquire when you realise what it will cost, then maybe we can get back to our holiday," Bert conceded.

"So that's a yes then," I asked in confirmation.

"Yes, okay, we'll stop by at the agent's first thing in the morning and then we can go on to Frobisher Hall which sounds as if it is well worth a visit. It will be much more interesting than some old ruin."

First thing in the morning directly after breakfast, I reminded Bert about his promise to take me into town and visit the estate agents dealing with Windrush Manor House.

"Okay, okay," he said, feeling a little badgered, "We'll stop off in town before going on to Frobisher Hall."

"Thank you, thank you," I said making a bit of a fuss of him to make up for the bullying. By nine thirty we had set off in the car for another day out and on the way, we pulled into town and I kept an eye out for the estate agents.

Chapter Two

"I see the agent, it's over there we can park outside," I said to Bert pointing out the premises. We pulled up outside and Bert held the agent's door open for me to go in first. Behind the desk was a young girl about twenty polishing her nails as she waited for customers. She looked up from her hands and said:

"Good Morning what can I do for you?"

"We are interested in Windrush Manor, which we believe is on your books," I said, fearing she may inform us it is already sold. Much to my surprise, she said the opposite.

"Oh yes, we haven't had an inquiry about Windrush Manor for ages, are you interested in buying the property?"

"We might," I replied, "If the price is right. Can you tell us what the owner wants for the property?" The young girl shook her hands vigorously drying her nails before wading into a pile of folders.

"Ah, here it is," the girl announced opening the folder. According to this, you will need to make an offer to the owner," she said apologetically.

The problem," I informed her, "is, we haven't the slightest clue what the property is worth."

Can you give us a ballpark figure?" Bert asked interjecting. The girl thought about Bert's question for a second and replied.

I'll ask Mr Bell, excuse me, I will just nip into his office, I won't be a second." The girl disappeared behind a glass door and moments later returned with a tall, slim gentleman.

Hello," he said, "I am Mr Bell. I understand you're interested in Windrush Manor and want a rough guide to its worth."

Yes, " I replied if you can give us a rough idea of what price it will fetch, then we can negotiate with the owners," I said, fearing it would be completely out of our pocket.

"Well," Mr Bell replied after a moment's thought. "I shouldn't be telling you this, but this property has been on the market for nearly five years, so I would expect the owners would be open to any sensible offer just to get the property off their hands."

"What would be a sensible offer?" Bert asked

"Let me see," Mr Bell pondered, "let's say in the region of £900,000."

"That cheap," I interjected.

"It needs a considerable amount of work, it is also a listed building so it can't be knocked down for housing, it can only be refurbished to its former glory using approved materials. I think before we go any further," the man cautioned, " being listed means it has to be restored to certain guidelines which will add to the overall costs of repairs. The guidelines dictate what can be restored both inside the property and outside. You can't just do what you want with it, it has to be restored to its former state."

We pondered over the prospect and Bert was about to leave, but I interrupted by saying to Mr Bell:

"We would like you to submit an offer of £700,000, can you do that for us please?"

"Yes, surely," Mr Bell answered, "Mabel will take down your details and I will get back to you in a few days when I have had a reply from the owners." We proceeded to give the young girl our details and we left the agents to go to the Frobisher Hall for a visit. When we were walking around Frobisher Hall, I annoyed Bert because all I could talk about was Windrush Manor.

Our holiday came to an end and we returned to our home in Weybridge Surrey and got on with our mundane lives. I worked from home designing software. Bert had an office in town and was a draftsman. Every Wednesday Isabel our slave would visit to give the house a good clean, which I would inspect before she went home and if it wasn't good enough I would punish her. It wasn't all punishment we would reward our sissy from time to time, but she needed to be reminded of her lowly place occasionally. I also enjoyed punishing her it made me feel so powerful to have her bend to my will. There isn't a greater trust one person can give to another than allow their Mistress to give them physical punishment.

I had almost forgotten about Windrush Manor and assumed as we had heard nothing about our offer, it was far too low and was dismissed out of hand. I accepted it was a daft idea, even if our offer was accepted where would we lay our hands on £700,000 let alone find the money for repairs which might twice as much again?

Therefore, I wasn't too disappointed not to hear anything more.

Nevertheless, a few days passed and out of the blue yonder, I did get a call from Mr Bell. I didn't recognise his voice and it took a few seconds to realise who was calling and for what reason.

"Good morning, Mrs Monroe, how are you this morning? I am calling to advise you your offer of £700.000 has been accepted by the owners of Windrush Manor. If you would like to give this some thought and if you would like a viewing we can arrange one at your convenience." This news brought all the excitement back to the fore and I wanted the Manor at any cost.

"Yes, I said, it would be prudent to have another good look at the house's interior before we make a firm offer as we haven't had a chance to look at the building properly yet. Please, could we come up for a viewing on Saturday?" I asked.

"Yes, of course, just drop into our offer when you arrive, I shall be here to show you around the manor and discuss things further." Mr Bell said before ringing off.

I had a hell of a job getting Bert to agree to go back to Kent on Saturday, but I persisted and for the sake of an easy time, he agreed. In the meantime, I looked at different ways to raise the cash for the purchase. I managed to get pledges from other members of the B.D.S.M., community in return for a share of the house. As I envisaged the manor becoming a business, it was important for Bert and I, to retain at least 51% outright ownership. We achieved this by crowdfunding, venture capital, equity release, loans from friends and using our life savings.

This is very half-baked," Bert remarked. "What sort of business do you intend to run a hotel or something?" He asked over breakfast one morning.

I have lots of ideas," I replied, "But one step at time, let's look at the property again on Saturday before we make any firm decisions. I am confident I can raise the capital to buy and I have ideas on how we can do the necessary repairs on the cheap."

How do we do that?" Bert asked.

We use slaves in the B.D.S.M., community, there are enough slaves out there with the skills we need as an incentive we can give each helper a handful of shares in the property. Many will be happy to work for us without any recompense, after all, they are slaves who will be just happy to help and be bullied and whipped occasionally."

"Okay," Bert agreed reluctantly, "Let's decide after we have had another good look at the property." I knew secretly Bert intended to put me off on Saturday after viewing the property, there was no way he wanted to buy it, but I had already decided the manor house would be mine, hook or by crook regardless of what Bert wanted.

Chapter Three

We drove up to Kent, Friday night and stopped in a Bed and Breakfast and after breakfast, on Saturday morning we drove into town and arrived at the estate agent at 10 O'clock.

Mr Bell was there on his own waiting for our arrival. He came out of the office to greet us and whilst he was locking the estate agent's door he asked:

"Are we using my car or yours?"

"You may as well come in ours," I replied. Mr Bell had a thick folder with him and happily climbed into the back of our car. We drove to the manor house and parked close to the huge front door.

"Right we'll have a quick walk around the grounds first, considering the house has been empty for some time the grounds aren't too overgrown and won't take much to have all look nice and neat again. The grounds cover an area of one hectare, which is a lot of land in this area," said Mr Bell.

I didn't speak as we walked around but I saw all sorts of potential for the grounds and was becoming more and more enthused. Finally, we arrived back at the front door after circumnavigating the outside of the property. Although tiles were missing and windows that needed replacing and some rotting timber, it wasn't actually too horrendous and it wouldn't take that much to remedy. It was now time to look inside again.

Inside the property was a different story the grand staircase was completely rotten and would need to be replaced in its entirety. It would also need to be replaced under the rules for a listed property we would not be able to use a cheaper alternative even if we wanted to. I also noticed many of the floorboards throughout the house were also rotten as were several window frames and there were signs of rising dampness. The house also needed rewiring and a modern heating system.

With a quick tot up in my mind it would take £500,000 to renovate at commercial rates, we may be able to do the job far cheaper using our community members. Bert made things out to be far worse than they really were to put me off, to no avail, I might add, this house had my name written all over it. When we returned home, I rang Mr Bell and put in a formal offer which was accepted, now we just had to wait for the lawyers to do their thing and Windrush Manor House will be ours. I admit when I made a formal offer I did tremble a bit, realising what I had let myself in for. Bert may be right, it is total madness.

Soon the house was ours, we employed an army of slave helpers to work on the house. It wasn't long before the house began to look like it was in its formal glory. The house was coming alive again after a long sleep. Bert and I lived on-site in a 35-foot static caravan which we sited close to the entrance, but shielded by trees so it didn't look out of place or too unsightly. When the property was about half finished I invited Christine a Mistress friend of mine over to see how we were progressing, she stopped with us in the caravan for a weekend. It was autumn now, but still hot and sunny and we had tables and chairs outside for use on nice days. The weekend Christine visited was one of those nice late summer weekends.

Bert, Christine and I sat around a table outside and watched workers repairing some of the window frames. Christine was the salt of the earth, a charming lady in her early forties and very elegant and needless to say quite dominant and had her own slaves and spoke well with a polished voice.

"This will be a lovely house when you're finished," Christine said whilst sipping her drink and admiring the building, "but how are you going to pay for all this work and the ortgage?" she asked with concern. "It must be osting you both an arm and a leg?"

Stately homes manage it," I said, " by turning he estate into a business. We are presently hinking on the lines of a theme park, or ossibly an upmarket hotel and conference entre."

Um," Christine uttered whilst thinking, "have ou thought about something associated with he B.D.S.M., community?" she asked.

I can see you have something in mind," I observed. "What ideas do you have?" I asked I would like to hear them as we are open to good uggestions."

Well, it will have to be something you enjoy doing to be a success, or you'll get bored with it after a time and cease to put in your best efforts," she said as thought about the matter. "I know you have your own slave. I believe she is a sissy maid?" Asked Christine.

"Yes, that's right her name is Isabel. She's not here today she is at home, making sure the house is clean for our return, She is a very loya slave I wouldn't be without her," I said wondering what Christine had in mind.

"Then why don't you start a school for sissy maids. You have the relevant experience, space ample facilities everything. I'm sure many Mistresses will be happy to come and offer you their services for just food and a roof over their head. Then you'll have everything you need staff, plus an ongoing army of domestics to keep this large house clean. You can charge them for the privilege which will, overtime, pay for the repairs, heating and taxes. It is a win, win situation," added Christine. "With the right marketing," she continued, " I reckon it will be a success and if it doesn't make enough money for your overheads, you can incorporate other ideas based on the community to run alongside the sissy academy."

"Yes, you're right Christine," I replied. "I could also build a dungeon and hire it out as a sideline. There must be loads of things I can do, but I do like the idea of training sissy maids. I can call it Bridget Monroe's finishing school for sissies" I added getting quite enthused and excited.

The conversation with Christine had sealed my fate, Windrush Manor was going to become an academy for budding sissy maids. I'll be able to train sissies in all the skills a sissy needs, deportment, all aspects of domestic work, silver service and much more. At the end of their training, they will get a certificate and will keep a list of Mistresses who want a fully-trained sissy so we can refer our best newly trained graduates.

Another month went by and the furniture arrived. No tat, this house deserved decent furniture and it would be something for the trainee sissies to polish and keep clean. Finally, Bert and I moved in and we watched our caravan being towed away. Our last really big expense was for specialist bespoke furniture for the dungeon, most were made lovingly and specifically for us by members of the community.

Chapter Four.

Now the reality was slowly beginning to settle in as bills for all the repairs begin to fall on our doormat. I set aside a south-facing room to become my office. Setting up a comfortable office seemed a priority as there was no time to lose getting the house operating as a viable business. One of the first things I did was to set aside a week with Bert's help to design and set up a website for Bridget Monroe's finishing school for sissies. The website had only been up for hours and I was already getting loads of enquiries.

I wasn't ready to book any sissies just yet as I needed a handful of willing Mistresses to, live in, and become teachers, each eventually having their own class of sissies to train. I would take the role of a Matron and oversee all the training and discipline wayward and unruly sissies.

I was also surprised at the number of Mistresses who had applied for the five jobs on offer. I stressed there would be no wages, just accommodation, food, light and heat and plenty of sissies to train. The lack of employment opportunities and benefits hadn't put Mistresses off and we had plenty of interest in the posts. Therefore, I set aside a couple of days to interview potential Mistresses. I felt it was important to have people here we were all likely to get along with. The more harmony the better things will run and we'll have a better chance of making the endeavour a success.

Over two and a half days we interviewed twenty Mistresses who were interested in the posts we offered. Out of the twenty we chose five whom I felt were willing to follow a curriculum that I will set out. I also wanted Mistresses who had experience dealing with sissies as opposed to submissives. I felt from my own experience sissies are a breed unto themselves and have different needs from other submissives. They need to be treated differently from some slaves s they tend to be very gentle individuals and eed to be handled with care.

verything was now quickly taking shape. The ouse looked the part I wanted to convey, an xpensive and well-appointed manor house fit to eceive a queen. The house will need an army of aying sissies to keep it up to scratch and that vas what I intended to find. The website I had et up also attracted a large number of fakes and me wasters, we quickly got around this roblem, before we booked any sissies we asked or a small refundable deposit before we would alk seriously, which quickly ruled out those vho were not serious about coming. We didn't lave time to waste assisting people's fantasies by pandering to their emails, that is not what we ure here for.

Our first intake was twelve sissies. We arranged for them to all show up on the same day. The idea being we could train them all at the same pace and have a graduation party on the same day they leave as fully-trained sissies. We began by offering one week's training. Two weeks would have been better and we decided to offer an intermediate course for any sissies who wanted to stay another week. However, we thought two weeks would be too expensive for some and put them off so we decided on one week as a default. As we are short of staff with the first intake we decided to offer five of the best sissy's permanent posts as housemaids for the manor, under similar terms to that of a Mistress, except their accommodation would be in the form of a dormitory and not a single room which the Mistresses enjoyed. Needless to say, they will also be expected to work twelve hours a day without any time off. You'll be surprised how many trained sissies jumped at the chance to be our full-time housemaids.

I had arranged for a coach to collect our trainee sissies from the railway station. A couple came by car, but they had to wait in a room for the remainder of the trainees to arrive so we could address them as a group at the same time. The coach was due to arrive at four PM and I was getting all excited at the prospect and paced up and down my little office as I impatiently waited for our first intake of sissies to arrive.

The coach finally pulled into the drive. I heard from my office a vehicle cutting through the gravel and stopping at the manor's front door. I raced to the top of the stairs and looked down on the foyer and watched through the opened door as the driver began to unload cases from the back of the coach to a small gaggle of potential sissy maids.

All the sissies before coming to the manor had to supply and buy their own maid's uniform.

Although it meant an additional cost to the sissy we felt it best if the uniform were all the same and we insisted on an Edwardian maid's uniform which the sissy could buy online before their course. We recommended a site which made handmade dresses and we also got a small commission for each dress. We didn't think a French maid's uniform appropriate for a manor house and was too frivolous. Our maids will get real training and should be dressed as real maids.

All twelve sissies had assembled in the foyer as the coach left. I came down the new grand staircase as slowly and as dignified as I could. I wanted to be clear to my new pupils I was the most senior Mistress and the bee's knees, someone to be revered and respected.

"Gather together in a semi-circle I wish to talk to you all," I shouted in my most polished voice as I reached the bottom of the staircase. "I am Bridget Monroe the patron of this establishment and you each may call me Matron." I paused for effect and scanned my new and first entry of sissies. I could see they were all terrified about what was to become of them. To think everyone had paid for this privilege to be taken way out of their comfort zone. I was determined not to disappoint them and for each to think it was money well spent and they will go away well-trained as competent sissy maids and ready at any task put before them.

"First before we continue," I added having surveyed the group, it is important for each of you to feel in the role. So I suggest the staff show you each to the dormitory and you can change into your new uniforms and gather back here in twenty minutes to discuss things further."

I left the group to disperse and head off to their dormitory. I in the meantime retreated to my office and had a cup of lukewarm coffee while I waited for my new trainees to assemble again in the foyer. When I returned to the foyer it was like a dream that had come true. Each sissy looked a picture in their full-length Edwardian uniforms, each pupil bore a well-pressed white apron and a little frilly cap. I felt as if I had regressed into the beginning of the twentieth century and I was the lady of the house surveying my staff.

"There is no need to panic or worry, today is a free day," I reassured the group. "You'll all be tired from your travels and we won't be expecting anything from you for the remainder of today. Soon you'll be shown to the food hall where you'll be fed dinner. Tomorrow morning at six AM, you'll assemble in Classroom Number One, where you'll be called one by one or your initial interview. At the interview, you'll be given a name tag which you'll wear so we can get to know each of you by name."

Tomorrow will be a fairly easy day for you too, as it will mostly comprise of administration. Your course will run for one week with an option of an advanced training course which will run for another week if you will like to make use of it. All students will leave with a certificate they can show a prospective Mistress." "Although this is a new business, we expect to quickly establish a good reputation which many Mistresses and Masters will come to respect. I will now leave you in the hands of Mistress Alexia," I said, retreating back into an adjacent room.

Head Mistress Alexia, lead the trainees off towards the food hall. After the pupils have eaten, they will be allowed to rest for the remainder of the day to recover from their travels as many had come hundreds of miles to be with us.

Chapter Five

I can't say I was delighted to get up, dressed an fed by six AM. I was not a morning person, but I felt I should at least on the first day make an effort to be first to greet the new pupils. I was also to conduct the initial interviews. In the foyer was a bunch of very sleepy-looking maids some I imagine wouldn't have had a wink of sleep being in a strange bed in a new environment. Some might have also been dreading what was to become of them.

So my first speech of the morning was to reassure the intake we would again be fairly gentle with them, but not to expect this to be the trend and that we will quickly be putting greater demands on each of the pupils.

After breakfast, the sissy maids assembled in classroom number one and awaited for their names to be called into an office where I was waiting to interview them. The interview was short but it allowed me to access each maid and it was a chance to be a little bit more personal as much of their training will be as a group. At the end of each interview, I reminded each maid she will be subject to punishment if her work did not reach the college standards and if they require serious discipline they will be sent to me, although the Mistress of the class can also dish out light to medium punishment, I will be reserved for more serious transgressions.

After the initial interviews were conducted I introduced the students to Mistress Viki who will be taking over the class. Mistress Viki was a young girl in her early twenties, slim as a rake, but very pretty with striking blue eyes and a personality to match. Viki despite being short and petite was no shrinking violet and was quite a disciplinarian and formidable when annoyed.

I left Mistress Viki to take over the class and I retreated to the far corner of the classroom to observe the proceedings without appearing to interfere. I wanted to access the class and Viki's performance.

"Right," Viki said, clapping her hands, let's stop chattering and come to attention. This morning we will be looking at your appearance. A maid needs to be well turned out and ready for a day's work. Mistresses will take a dim view if you appear for work slovenly and dishevelled. A maid must look her very best at all times."

'From now on you'll take extra special attention to your uniform, hair and makeup. Each of you will wear full makeup according to our guidelines. I hope you all had time to read the leaflet which was given to you last night before bed and have digested its content ready for today's lesson." Mistress paused to allow the class to absorb what she had said.

" All stand up," she bellowed. " I shall now walk amongst you and inspect your uniforms." Mistress Viki strutted down each row of desks inspecting the front and back of each sissy's uniform, murmuring and muttering as she went. On the third row, she stopped at a sissy and pulled a face.

"What's your name?" she asked loudly, looking at her name tag. "Rose," she said before the sissy could answer go to the front of the class and wait for me." Mistress continued her inspection and then returned to Rose at the front of the class. "Rose do a twirl for me, I want to ask the other pupils what is wrong with your uniform." Rose obliged and did a nervous twirl if it could be called that.

"Any idea girls, what is wrong with Rose's uniform? Several hands went up, and Mistress chose one pupil to answer.

"It's her apron Mistress," replied the pupil, "it's not in a bow at the back."

"That's right," agreed Mistress Viki. "Girls, will you all turn around and show Rose how the apron should be tied at the back, according to the guidelines." All the girls briefly faced the other way to show Rose their apron bows on the back.

"Do you see Rose?" Mistress asked, "each maid has a nice big apron bow tied neatly at the back. Yours is just a rushed reef knot and could not be escribed as a bow of any description. Not only it an unsightly knot, but it will crease your pron so it will need to be ironed before each year." Mistress walked over and brought her hair and put it down in front of Rose. In her and Mistress had a cane which she collected from a hook on the classroom door.

Bend over," she demanded. "It is best to start s we mean to carry on. I am going to be cruel o be kind, later you'll thank me for this." With hose words, she brought the cane down brutally on poor Rose's bottom three times. Although punishment was over the girl's skirt they were full force and had Rose in tears and no doubt will have some serious marks to nurse for a few days despite her padding.

"Now go to your seat, I will expect better from you tomorrow," Mistress said. "If you can't make a bow you get someone to do it for you.

Now we will turn our attention to your make-up. Whilst we insist on full make-up there are some provisos, for example, no false eyelashes. You're domestic servants and you're not going to the Ball. Also, there will be no false nails, as you cannot scrub, wash up or clean whilst wearing false nails. Except for Rose, I am quite pleased with your turnout and now you may go to lunch. After lunch, we will turn our attention to maid deportment. Off you go and enjoy your lunch be back in this classroom in an hour sharp," Mistress said dismissing the class. When the class emptied I congratulated Viki for holding a good class and I would sit in for the afternoon session after I too had lunch.

After lunch Mistress Viki got all the pupils to move the desks to the side of the classroom just leaving the chairs. The pupils nervous sat back down in their chairs awaiting Mistress Viki for further instructions.

"Maids at this academy will be trained to the highest standards and will leave here with the skills to serve at the highest establishments. To achieve this each maid will need to learn graceful and feminine deportment. Both looking and behaving as feminine as you can is a must. Today we are going to start with the simple act of sitting on a chair." Mistress bellowed "Stand-up girls," when everyone stood up, she said, "now sit down." Mistress walked among the girls she tapped the arms of three sissies and said they had done well. "However, the rest of you were an absolute rabble."

"Someone bring me a chair," she barked. "A sissy ran over with a spare chair and put it in front of Mistress. Mistress turned the chair around to face the girls. "Now take special attention to the way I sit. I shall sit in slow motion so you can observe," she said as she sat down on the hard-backed chair. "You'll notice I sat on the chair without looking at it. Now watch me again in slow motion. I'll talk you through it. I glanced at the chair before sitting and I made a mental note of where it is. I back up to the chair without looking until I feel it touch my thighs. I now gracefully sit keeping my legs tightly together. You might also note, I only sit on the edge of the seat as this looks much more graceful and it is easier to stand back up again gracefully. Now girls, let's see you try." The pupils followed Mistress's example and Mistress seemed quite pleased with their efforts.

"Before we move on there is one more thing I want to say about the art of sitting and that is what to do with your knees. Now it isn't acceptable to show your knickers off, no matter how nice they are, and this is why we keep our legs together. This can be done in several ways, you can cross your feet over the knees, which can look very graceful, or you can adopt a Princess Kate's look and keep your knees tight together and slightly to the side which can also look very graceful indeed, the choice is yours. Don't forget to smooth your skirt as you sit, it will save it from getting creased unnecessarily. There are two ways to smooth your skirt, you can run your hands down the back of the skirt towards your knees, or you can smooth the skirt with your hands at the front by running them towards your knees whichever you find the easiest."

Mistress Viki got the girls to sit and they sat several times until she was satisfied with their performance.

"Right before we end the class, pupils I would like you to stand up," Mistress Viki said walking amongst the girls again. "Not one of you is standing properly, any idea what is wrong with the way you are all standing?" she asked pausing for a reply. All the sissies looked at each other and were at a loss at what they were doing wrong each wondering what the skill is in the simple act of standing up.

"I will tell you," Mistress said, standing to attention herself, "what is the difference between the way I stand and the way you are all standing?" she asked.

Again, all the sissies were clueless as to what they were doing wrong. A petite sissy called Mary put her hand up.

"Yes, Mary, speak up girl so we can all hear you," Mistress demanded.

"I think I have the answer," she said nervously.

"Well, go on," Mistress urged.

You're not standing with your feet together as we all are," she said, confident she had the right answer.

Yes, you're correct, but only partially right. I'm standing with one foot slightly in front of the other, this will give me a more graceful and slimmer outline. However, there is something else wrong with the way you are all standing any ideas?" She asked. "I'll put you out of your misery and tell you," she said. "Men stand with their arms rotated slightly inwards whilst girls' arms rotate slightly outwards," said Mistress giving a graphic demonstration. " We also walk this way, it's a small thing, but it all adds to giving you a feminine graceful look. The art of being feminine is a host of tiny differences to the way men behave which are often overlooked by budding sissies."

"Can any of you sissies tell me any other differences between a woman and a man?" Mistress Viki asked her audience. Before anyone could answer Mistress said:

"Women use different nuances than men. Can any of you think of an example? " She asked, looking around the room. The sissies seemed lost for any answers. "I'll tell you some, men tend not to use words like cute, sweet, gosh, wonderful and excited, these are just a few. Your homework tonight is to think about words that are generally used by women more than men."

"Now we'll go for a well-deserved coffee break. Before you leave," she added as some pupils were already at the door. "After your break, report outside the front door in your gym outfit for some physical exercise. A fit body means an active mind and an active mind means a sissy who is paying attention in class," Mistress added as the girls rushed out of the room.

Chapter Six

Whilst the pupils went for their coffee break Viki and I went to the staff room for our own break. In the staff room, we were greeted by two other Mistresses, Mistress Amber and Mistress Fiona. Both girls were in their mid-thirties and both had longish black hair. Both were deep in conversation and enjoying coffee and biscuits. As I entered with Viki, I said:

"I'm sorry we don't have classes for you yet, but soon our sissy intakes will get bigger as we promote the academy more."

"We were just discussing things before you came in Matron," said Mistress Fiona.

"Yes," interjected Mistress Amber, "Why don't we cater for 'pain sluts' as well as sissies. There is a nice big room opposite where we could install a couple of sofas for the Mistresses and some metal cages and torture equipment for the slaves."

"Then when we're not busy in class," added Mistress Fiona, "we could beat a few paying slaves to while away the time and have fun, of course."

"I'm sure there are plenty of takers out there who will be happy to pay to be whipped by an experienced and very cruel Mistress. It will keep us busy when things are slack and bring in extra revenue. I saw online there is a chateaux-type manor house in the Czech Republic, offering similar services for submissives, they have been going for years so it must pay well."

"That's a good idea," Viki said to me. "A couple of sofas and half a dozen cages of assorted sizes and a few torture implements won't break the bank and they will soon pay for themselves."

"When the slaves are not being caged and beaten, they can be put to work in the kitchen where we always need extra staff," added Mistress Fiona.

I took on board what the Mistresses said and just a few days later we had an extra arrow to our bow, and we had what we decided to call The Torture Room, up and running. This was distinct from the dungeon as it was in a more relaxed setting for the Mistresses, not the slaves. Within a week we had four "pain sluts" to occupy the new cages.

Those Mistresses who didn't have a class to run would amuse themselves by beating and caning hapless slaves. It wasn't long before we added a few wooden stocks to restrain slaves who were in for a severe beating. On the house grounds, we set a patch aside for all the building rubbish and broken furniture etcetera. When we accumulated a reasonable amount of rubbish we would hire someone to come out and collect it. Mistress Amber noticed in amongst the rubbish was a broken beer barrel from years gone by. We decided to have it repaired and now it is in the torture chamber and is used to bend slaves over for a good sound caning. An attempt at the navel enactment of "kissing the gunner's daughter".

Poor Bert felt left out with all the gorgeous dominant women around and kept mainly to our private quarters, of course, Bert, who was a natural dominant was into submissive women and found dominant women unnerving and intimidating. Bert offered to handle the ccounts and administration and preferred to spend most of his time in the office while I oversee the classes and other activities. After coffee, I went outside and saw Class Number One busy doing physical jerks. The physical training instructor was a buxom girl Mistress Crimson. I watched as she casually walked among the girls as they did knee-ups. If a sissy wasn't putting her knees up high enough, Mistress Crimson would stop and give the girl a hard stroke of her riding crop as encouragement which she seemed to enjoy immensely.

"That's it, girls," Mistress Crimson said, blowing her whistle and clapping her hands. "You may all go off to have a shower, change back into your uniforms and then report back to the classroom for further instruction."

All the girls ran off back into the building to the showers. They had fifteen minutes to shower before having to be back in class dressed in the uniforms where Mistress Viki anxiously waited for them to arrive.

"That's it, sissies," Mistress Vicki said as the girls trickled back, "take your seat and we'll wait for the others to come before continuing with your lessons." When all the girls arrived Mistress Viki read off the register to ensure all were in attendance. Each pupil had to raise their hand as their name was called out just like at school.

"A pupil is missing," Mistress Viki said in horror, looking down at the register she asked, "where is trainee maid Susan?" Just as Mistress Viki spoke in came Susan and she headed off towards her seat.

"No, don't sit at your desk," Mistress Viki barked, "Come out here to the centre of the class and explain to me why you are late?" The girl did as she was told and came and stood in front of her Mistress.

"Sorry Mistress," the hapless maid said. "I couldn't find my shoes."

"There are no excuses for lateness, none," Mistress said, pulling out a spare chair in the centre of the room. "On the classroom door hook, you'll see my cane, which I affectionately call my tickling stick, go and fetch it, please." The poor sissy knew what was going to happen next and slowly and reluctantly she went to the door to fetch the cane. She returned to Mistress's side and passed her the implement. Mistress Viki bent the cane right over to a point where it might have snapped. Mistress pointed with her eyes to the chair.

"You know what to do, bend over the back of the chair and grip the base hard as this is going to hurt," Mistress said slowly raising her skirt and tucking it in so it wouldn't fall during the proceedings. Then she ran her fingers inside the girl's knickers and lowered them slowly and ceremoniously to just below the buttocks.

"This is a lesson to you other girls, obedience is the name of the game. Susan's suffering will help you all to remember to arrive at class on time, every time, with no exceptions. Right, young lady, it is twelve strokes for you. I would like you to count them nice and loud and the class will count with you for encouragement. Only you Susan will say thank you after each stroke."

Mistress gave her tickling stick one last bend before placing the cane lightly on Susan's bottom before raising it and coming down hard on the poor girl's cheeks. Almost immediately an angry red welt appeared where the cane fell. A tearful Susan thanked Mistress before she administered the next stroke. The pupil was reduced to a mass of tears by the time the punishment had finished.

"Susan's misdemeanour has eaten into the next lesson, so we will crack on. Susan go and stand against the wall with your hands on your head until I tell you otherwise." Susan quietly whilst rubbing her bottom went to the classroom wall and stood there as told, with her hands on her head.

"This lesson is also about feminine deportment. If you have read your lesson notes properly, you will have brought to class both flat shoes and heels for this lesson," Mistress Viki eyed each of the students to ensure all had come with the right shoes as requested.

"Good, she said this lesson is all about walking femininely and gracefully. We'll start in the foyer. Follow me," Mistress said, heading for the classroom door. The group of sissies assembled at the foot of the grand staircase. "We'll start learning how to walk up and down stairs wearing heels. I shall walk up a few steps and down so you can observe how I am walking. I will demonstrate the art of going upstairs is completely different from coming downstairs."

Mistress began to ascend the staircase. "Note I am only putting the sole of the shoe only on each stair as I go. There is no need to put the heel on the stairs as you are ascending. It is important to hold the bannister to help maintain a good balance." Mistress went up about six of seven steps and turned in readiness to come back down. "Now you'll note I am turning my feet in slightly so I can put the whole of the shoe on each stair as I descend both the sole and the heel. This will give you much better balance and has the added effect of looking very graceful.

once again, do hold the bannister for both safety and effectiveness."

"Right Susan, you can come away from the wall now and join us. I am going to allow you to redeem yourself by going up the stairs first. I see you already have your heels on, good. As you didn't see me demonstrate I will go first and then it will be your turn."

Mistress gracefully walked up a few steps and down and indicated it was now Susan's turn. Poor Susan stumbled on the third step but managed slightly better coming down the stairs.

"Oh dear, oh dear," Mistress said tut-tutting, "Susan fetch the tickling stick right away this needs to be sorted." Susan scurried off and fetched the cane. She was made to bend over the third step and Mistress gave her three strokes over her skirt. "You will have a sore bottom by the time I have finished with you today young lady," Mistress said as she demonstrated again. Susan was made again to follow but managed a passable attempt and was allowed to return the tickling stick to its pride and place it on the classroom door. Then each of the pupils had to demonstrate they too could walk up and down stairs with grace.

"Next," Mistress Viki said "we'll practice walking around the foyer in flats and heels. I will go first," she said, slipping off her heels an putting on a pair of flat shoes. Mistress gave a demonstration. "The art is keeping the feet close together and taking small gentile steps, not big strides as most men make." This was an easy exercise and Mistress had the class walking around the foyer in circles until she was satisfied. Next, was showing the class how to walk in heels, which soon became apparent this was a different skill altogether.

"Watch me," Mistress said as she set off around the foyer. "Note I am again taking little steps, but this time I am placing one foot slightly in front of the other as if walking along a painted line on the floor, this looks much more graceful and has the added bonus of forcing the bum to wriggle in a feminine fashion."

"The class will now go and fetch their exercise books and bring them here in the foyer." When all the sissies returned Mistress went on to say. "Another way to look your most feminine is to stand up straight and not slouch. Men have a habit of slouching forward, especially when they are out walking. So each of you will place your exercise book on your head and we will repeat the exercises you have just learnt. We will start with flat shoes. Any books dropped will result in punishment." Each sissy balanced their exercise book on their head and set off in a circle around the big foyer. One by one a book would fall to the ground with an ominous clack.

"Leave the books on the floor," Mistress barked fetching back the tickling stick and placing it on the chair in the centre of the foyer. "One, two… five errant girls," Mistress said counting and pointing to the errant sissies. "Right, come here and stand in a row in front of the chair."

The girls did as they were told and had no doubts about what was going to happen to them. Mistress pulled the first errant sissy forward bent her over the chair and administered six rapid strokes, followed by the next girl and the next until they were all punished.

" Now let's see how you all fair wearing heels," Mistress instructed. Needless to say, nearly half dropped their books and now the punishment queue was long and winding, but it only took a couple of minutes for Mistress to deal with the offenders after each sissy endured a rapid caning.

"Right sissies, that's it for today," she said to her tearful pupils. "Tomorrow, if you look at your notes you'll assemble her in the foyer. Domestic duties will make up much of your working day as a sissy maid, so tomorrow you'll assemble here with floor cloths, detergent and mops and buckets. It will be time to show me how good you all are at domestic duties. You may go to the food hall now and get dinner and I will see each of you later." Mistress said, dismissing the class.

Chapter Seven

In the morning Mistress Viki and I arrived in the foyer to be greeted by a less-than-enthusiastic class of sissies. They looked a sight, all supporting their buckets and mops. I went over to a corner to watch the proceeding and allowed Mistress Viki to take charge of the cleaning duties.

"You, you and you," Mistress Viki said, tapping the shoulders of three girls, "you can stay here in the foyer. The remainder will assemble outside and your duties will be to pick up detritus which collects in the wind around the outside of the building," Mistress said, passing a bunch of grabbers and bin liners to one of the sissies to hand out.

The first group set about mopping the foyer floor somewhat half-heartedly. Mistress Viki was quick to see the lack of enthusiasm and stomped off to the classroom and returned with chair and her ticking stick. She didn't say a word, but put the chair right in the centre of the room with the cane on the chair seat so all could see it. This seemed to do the trick and the girls began to mop with more determination and gusto. Mistress walked around the room mumbling to herself.

You're not getting into the corners properly, we need to start again," she said seeming a little bit annoyed.

What clean the whole floor again," said one of the sissies. Mistress just stood silently for a second or two looking at the sissy with incredulous eyes.

"Well, you have a choice Daisy," Mistress said reading her name tag. "You and, the other girls mop the floor again taking special care of the corners, or take turns bending over the chair I brought into the room, your choice, what will it be? I am more than happy to cane you if that is what you prefer and you'll still have to clean th corners afterwards?"

"We'll mop," Daisy said not relishing a session bent over the chair.

"Good, I am being extra kind to you today, so don't spoil it." Mistress left the girls to mop and went outside. She quickly returned to the foyer with a protesting pupil which she held by her ear. "Attention girls," Mistress shouted, "stop what you are doing. I went outside and what was the first thing I saw, but this errand girl standing against a wall smoking in plain sight."

Mistress roughly bent the girl over the chair and equally roughly removed her skirt and panties. "You may witness this girl's punishment, in case any of you fancy a smoke outside when we change over duties later on," she said picking up the cane and giving it a compulsory bend. "This is a serious offence, one short of being reported to the Matron. I shall give this girl eighteen strokes which I am sure will make her think twice about smoking outside of official break times."

The foyer filled with the echo of a cane crashing down on the sissy's bare bottom. Soon the cane sounds were joined by pleading, begging and crying. The audience looked on with grim faces as the last of the strokes were administered. The girl was told to stand and straighten her dress. The sissy wobbled to her feet with tears streaming down her face as she pulled up her knickers and straightened her skirt. "You may return outside and I'll check later to ensure you're hard at work, that is unless you'll like another session over the chair today."

The mop brigade was sent off with the mops and buckets to return to the foyer with two mechanical polishers.

"You'll take one polisher to each end of the room. It will be a bit like mowing the grass you'll polish the floor in straight lines. Only when the floor gleams can you stop and call me over to sign off your work. The machines cannot get tight into the corners so the spare sissy will have to polish the corners by hand," clapping to indicate she wanted the girls to start work.

Mistress Viki went back outside this time to check if the errant maid was hard at work, Mistress smiled when she saw the girl filling a bin liner with rubbish. She slowly walked around the perimeter of the building to ensure no rubbish remained around the grounds. She seemed satisfied and allowed the girls to take a break in the weak sunshine for a few minutes. She then allowed the mop brigade to come outside and join the other sissies in a short break. I called Mistress Viki over to me where I sat on a bench with a flask of coffee.

"I think you deserve a drink," I said, pouring Viki a beaker of coffee from my flask. "It's nice and hot I have just made it," I reassured her as I passed her the cup. "I am very pleased with the way you are running your classes," I said, "we would like to offer you a permanent position, do you accept?" I asked fearfully of the reply. It was a must in the business to secure the services of good teachers and Viki met that criterion amply and therefore would be reluctant to lose her to another academy.

"Yes, I would love to stay on," Viki replied. "I am enjoying my work and there are lots more to teach the sissies yet, we have barely started their education."

"Good," I replied, "we can't have too many teachers like you," I replied, and then we turned our attention to watching the girls enjoy their break. We decided to release the girls for the remainder of the day as we felt they deserved it.

"In the morning girls," Mistress said, as the sissies were dispersing, "assemble in the kitchen, not the classroom, do you understand?" Mistress waited for a few replies and nods as the sissies disappeared back into the building. The next morning I joined Mistress Viki in our big commercial-sized kitchen. When all the girls assembled Mistress asked:

"Who can cook?" as she eyed the group. All enthusiastically put their hands up without exception. "That's good to see," replied Mistress approvingly. "Then you'll need no further instruction from me, each of you will make a chicken pie. You'll see all the ingredients on the table and I'll be back in an hour or two to inspect each of your pies after they have been baked in the oven. If they are not good enough, I have a very special treat for transgressors."

Viki and I went off to The Torture Room to see what was going on. Mistress Ruby had a skinny slave bent over our recycled beer barrow. She was using a single-tailed whip and had been whipping the slave for some time as his backside was like a piece of raw meat.

Another Mistress had a slave walking around with a testicle restraint on. This testicle restraint consisted of two pieces of wood with two large screw threads and butterfly clips, which could be used to screw the two pieces of wood down on the slave's balls behind his legs, preventing him from standing up. This device is also known as a humbler. The slave had to walk bent over double and had been doing so for over an hour. Another slave had a Mistress standing over him pouring candle wax onto his back.

We stopped to chat and have coffee with a couple of unoccupied Mistresses before returning to the kitchen. Before us was a line of baked chicken pies. Mistress examined each before picking up a fork and sampling a few. Each pie had a note of the sissy who baked it.

"Not bad," Mistress said, "cooking will also be duties for some of you depending on your new Mistress's wants and needs. There were a couple of pies which looked more like puddings. Sissy Mavis and Sissy Lucy to the front and receive your special punishment." The errant girls obliged and came out to the front of the kitchen.

"As we are assembled in the kitchen we're going to have a domestic punishment. It may not come as a surprise to some of you, but the kitchen has many a tool that can double as a punishment implement. Today, I'm going to settle on a large wooden spoon and a fly swat."

"Right you two naughty girls bend over the sink, pull up your skirts and remove your panties." When the sissy did as instructed Mistress gave each girl several hard strokes of the spoon. The girls protested and wriggled. "If you think that hurt, you had better brace yourselves, the fly swat will be much worse." Mistress was quite right the fly swat reduced both girls to a sobbing mess.

"Next time," Mistress Viki said before dismissing the two punished girls, " if you can't cook say so and I will help you. No you girls you can't leave the kitchen in this mess, before you leave to go to dinner, you'll need to clean all the surfaces and mop the floor. I'll check your work in the morning."

On the fourth morning of the sissy course, we upped the pace a bit as they were now over halfway through the course. Whilst Mistress Viki took the roll call I went into the Torture Room to see what was going on. Although it had barely turned seven o'clock there were already three slaves and three Mistresses in attendance. This room was barred to the sissies and the slaves would enter from a different entrance so the two groups never mixed or saw each other.

Slaves who desired severe punishment were a different breed from a sissy and we felt the two shouldn't mix. We also thought if the sissies saw the slaves being punished and tortured, they might leave thinking that might be their ultimate fate. The worst a sissy will get is a caning or time out and other subtle humiliations, a slave by contrast, would get the severest of beatings sometimes lasting up to an hour or more. Some would leave the torture room bleeding from their punishment. It sounds excessive, but they have paid for the privilege and many slaves would rebook for more of the same before leaving the manor.

When I stepped into the room, the first thing I saw was a middle-aged man who had neglected his body bent over the beer barrow we salvaged from the rubbish a few days before. Mistress Ruby, a lively, skinny wisp of a girl in her late twenties was wading into the slave with a long thin riding crop. She seemed to be thoroughly enjoying herself. She was finishing off the session and was giving her victim his last few strokes. When Mistress finished, she rubbed the poor man's tortured backside with her warm soft hands.

"You may go," she said to the slave, "I expect to see you at the same time tomorrow for more of the same. You're a good slave it is a pleasure to beat you. You may leave now," she added in a more authoritative voice. I watched her then strut over to a big cage which housed three hapless slaves.

"Which shall I choose next," she murmured.

"Eeny meany, miny moe,

Catch a slave by his toe,

If he hollers let him go.

Eeny, meany, miny moe."

"You," she barked pointing her finger and shouting to a skinny teenager, "come here to the cage door," she demanded opening the door for the terrified slave to pass through.

You're a very lucky boy having Mistress Ruby choose you next for my attention. Go over to the wooden stocks," she demanded, pointing to the particular stock she wanted to use. As Mistress secured the teenager's feet, arms and head in the device, she said:

I am not sure how far we can go with you, you don't look as if you can take much of a beating, but let's see, we'll start off gently to see how you go." Once the teenager was trusted and unable to move a muscle Mistress went off to the rack of whips.

"Um, what whip shall we start with," she said loud enough for her selected slave to hear. "I'm spoilt for choice, lets' start with a dressage whip and see if you like that." Mistress unpinned a long, thin dressage whip from the rack and went over to a clear space in the room and did a few practice shots with the whip at a bean bag. Once satisfied with her choice she came back over to her slave. She showed him the whip, "we'll sta: with this," she said, watching the boy grimace : the sight of the implement. She put the whip in the boy's mouth while she gently massaged the slave's back and buttocks.

"Is that nice," she purred. "All this attention from a beautiful goddess, you're so lucky," she added taking the whip from the slave's mouth. "Now you have had a good chance to see the whip, let's see what it feels like, are you ready? she asked.

With those words the room filled with the cracking sound of the whip quickly followed by a scream as the implement landed on the boy's back. A red mark appeared almost instantly.

"Don't be such a sissy," Mistress Ruby teased, "we have barely gotten started you'll get to know this whip well by the time I have finished with you. You may count the remaining strokes," insisted Mistress as she landed the next lash. Then Mistress picked up the pace and the whip seemed to be constantly in motion and the room filled with the sound of a cracking whip. The slave slouched in the wooden frame and Mistress stopped whipping and came forward and massaged the boy's wounds.

"How long are you here for?" Mistress asked.

"The weekend," the slave replied.

"In that case, you are reserved for me. If another Mistress wants to beat you, you say you are Mistress Ruby's slave. I will see you tomorrow after you have had a rest," she said, undoing the boy's bonds and letting him out of the contraption.

"I think there is time for one more slave to beat before I go off for a rest myself," said Mistress Ruby returning to the cage. "You the one with the ginger hair come forward to the cage door, I think we will finish off by giving you a good beating."

The slave stood up from a kneeling position and slowly came over to the door. Mistress opened it and grabbed the slave by his ear. "Come with me," she said going off towards the array of punishment contraptions. "Which shall we put you in," she mused as she surveyed each item of torture equipment. "I know we will put you on the St Andrews Cross. You're privileged that the cross only arrived this morning you'll be the first to use it. It rotates as well," Mistress said, spinning the device. The poor slave watched it go round and round until the device slowly cranked to a stop. "Right, let's have you on it step forward with your front to the cross," she said as she began to tie his feet and hands in a spread eagle position.

Mistress then went to the implement rack to choose her whip. "What shall we use next," she murmured to herself. "This thick leather tawse looks good," as she unpinned it from the rack. "Oh yes, she said approvingly," it's made from thick cowhide and has a six-inch pleat in it, so each stroke will be worth two." Mistress Ruby swished it several times as she returned to the cross and the waiting slave. "Let's see how you like this," she said striking the slave's buttocks without any warning. I saw his bottom quiver like a blancmange with the force of the strap. The hardened slave quickly lets out a loud agonising yelp.

"Matron," Mistress Ruby said, spotting me quietly standing in the corner, "would you like to have a go at disciplining this slave?" She asked holding out the tawse. I stopped to think about the proposition and I thought, well, why not and I stepped forward and took the tawse from Mistress's hand.

I bent the implement backwards and forwards a few times to get an idea of its severity. I was surprised at how thick and solid the strap is. I then approached the slave and backhanded him a swipe with the strap across the buttocks and watched as a thick white stripe appear instantly turning crimson and the slave quivering from the impact. I felt extremely powerful wielding the tawse and soon was flaying the slave in rhythm and enjoyed seeing the slave wriggle and squirm with each stroke as he pulled against his restraints. I was surprised at how much I had enjoyed myself.

"I'm sorry," I said to Mistress Ruby, "I seemed to have done your job for you, I don't think he can take much more."

No worries," Mistress Ruby replied, taking the cane back from me. "My arms were getting tired from a morning of beating slaves and they needed a rest. I think he can manage a few more strokes, though," Mistress Ruby decided as she laid into the slave once more until he was crying out in tears. "Now he has had enough," she said, releasing him and we didn't spin the cross once."

Chapter Eight

I left the Torture Room and returned to Mistress Viki in classroom number one. She was busy teaching the sissies to raise their voices to a feminine pitch with the aid of a laptop and some voice recording software. I took a chair at the back of the class and watched on. Mary a short chubby sissy began to swear in frustration because she couldn't get the software to work as she wanted. Unfortunately, she swore in hearing distance of Mistress Viki, who stomped over to the girl and stood before her with her arms on her hips.

"What did I just hear you say?" Mistress asked in an annoyed voice.

"Sorry Mistress but I can't get the software to work," Mary replied.

"It isn't the software, it is you, you're too stupid to use it properly. However, that isn't why I came over. "Girls" Mistress shouted to the class in a commanding voice, can any of you tell me what this sissy has done wrong?" Mistress added waiting for a reply.

"She swore," answered a voice from the back of the class.

"That's right, Mary swore. Sissies in this academy do not swear, ever. No Mistress or Master will take you on if you have a mouth like a sewer. It is a cardinal sin and will be punished severely. All sissies go to the washroom now and wait for me and Mary to arrive," Mistress demanded as she dismissed the class. When all the sissies had left the class Mistress Viki took something from her desk drawer and said to Mary:

"We will go and join the others, shall we,"

Mistress took the lead. I too was curious as to what punishment Mistress Viki had planned and followed on behind Mary and Mistress. When we entered the washroom where all the sissies were chatting.

"Silence," Mistress bellowed. "Girls form a semi-circle around this wash basin,"

The sissies did as requested and Mistress pushed Mary through the cordon and up to the basin.

"Can any of you sissies tell me what happens to wicked maids who use foul language."

"I think I can guess," said a sissy in the middle of the semicircle.

"Go on, let's hear what you think the suitable punishment should be?" Mistress Viki asked.

"You're going to wash her mouth out with soap," the sissy said confidently.

"Yes, Megan," Mistress replied reading her name tag, "you're right, in my pocket," she said producing a new bar of dark green soap, "I have a bar of carbolic soap for just such occasions."

"Step up to the basin Mary, we're going to cleanse your mouth and it will be a warning to any other sissy who is tempted to swear in my class. Open your mouth wide," Mistress said running the tap. Mary refused and Mistress helped the girl by holding her nose until she reluctantly opened her mouth. Mistress soaked the bar of soap under the tap and with the sissy struggling furiously as she wiped around the girl's mouth until the sissy collapsed coughing and choking in a tearful heap on the floor.

"Are you going to ever swear again Mary?" asked Mistress Viki. Between gasping, crying and choking the maid replied:

"No Mistress."

"Then we shall return to the classroom and begin our next lesson," Mistress said leaving the washroom. Back in the classroom Mistress clapped and brought the chatting class to attention. "It is time for our next lesson. How many girls can curtsey properly? If you can put your hand up." Several hands went up. "Go on girls come out to the front of the class, let's see your curtsey." The sissies curtseyed for Mistress.

"Um, not too bad an effort, but you all need improving. I will demonstrate but be warned this will be the first and last time I shall ever curtsey to a ravel like you, so pay close attention," Mistress said.

"I'll lift my skirt so you can see, I will place one leg slightly behind the other. Then I will hold lightly the skirt at the sides and dip bending my knees slightly and quickly return to the upright position. Now it is your turn sissies," she said waiting to see their efforts. Some grasped it immediately, others looked awkward and slow, so Mistress had them all come out the front of the class and stand in a row and curtsey repeatedly. Mistress walked up and down the line dismissing those who had grasped the concept, leaving those who were slow to get their curtsey right by continuing to practice for up to an hour until all were dismissed.

"That was a good effort," Mistress said, "I am pleased with you all and there was no reason for any of you to visit my tickling stick. Now pupils under what circumstances does a maid need to curtsey? She asked the class awaiting lots of replies.

"When entering a room," said one.

"When leaving a room," said another pupil.

"Any other occasions," Mistress asked the class.

The girls seemed clueless, so Mistress helped them out.

"How about, when a Master or Mistress addresses a maid?" The pupils agreed and Mistress went on to the next stage of the lesson. "Curtseying is an important part of a maid's protocol. However, there is more. When you have served your Mistress or Master and haven't been dismissed, you'll curtsey and step backwards occasionally glancing to see where the door is and stand by the door with your head bowed down and your hands demurely folded across your apron. Here you will stay no matter how long until you're needed again or dismissed. We shall practice, you," Mistress shouted to a girl at one of the front desks, come out here and show me what I have just discussed. Come and stand in front of me." The sissy left her desk and stood in front of Mistress

"You may assume you have just served me with a tray of coffee. I haven't dismissed you from the room what do you do? Show me," Mistress demanded. The girl started to go backwards.

"Don't forget to curtsey first," Mistress said, reminding the girl of her error. The sissy gave a nice curtsey and went slowly back to the door and stood there as Mistress had described.

"Good girl," Mistress said, clapping, "excellent effort. Now the next girl let's see you do the same." Mistress one by one went through the entire class; only needing to stop to cane one girl who had got the whole sequence wrong and clearly hadn't paid attention and paid the price for daydreaming with an extended session with the tickling stick.

I left Mistress Viki with her class and decided to go off to the office and see what Bert was up to. When I entered the office, Bert looked up at me with a worried look.

"What's the matter," I asked, sitting on Bert's knee and lighting a cigarette for him. I didn't smoke myself, but I enjoyed lighting his cigarettes occasionally.

"The books aren't balancing if we don't watch it we'll have a cash flow problem. We need extra revenue if we are going to survive." Bert said in a voice that conveyed he wasn't too optimistic about our chances of ever reaching our financial goals.

"I have some ideas, well, at least two ideas for being in extra cash," I said, passing Bert an ashtray and putting it in front of him. Bert drew on the last of the cigarette and stubbed it into the ashtray and asked:

"What do you have in mind?"

"Well, one of the Mistresses said the other day we are wasting the lovely grounds and we should hold monthly pony races." It is a two-arrowed bow, in as much as we can charge for being entered into the races and we can rent rooms for those who travel too far to go home the same day. There will be spectators too who will be spending in the beer tent and some of them will hire rooms. We could also entice more people to stop over if the event covered a whole weekend."

"That's an idea," Bert said I'll research it and sort out some prices and fees. The other idea?" He asked, taking more interest.

"Well, we have lots and lots of rooms just sitting empty," I replied, "which we could rent out to like-minded couples and singles who want to get away and enjoy a safe environment for a weekend or a holiday. As an inducement, we could give them free access to our new dungeon and Torture Room. That's for starters, I may come up with more moneymaking ideas, now I know it is important to improve our cash flow."

"Good," Bert said decisively, "we shall need all the revenue we can get".

"I have another idea, it has just come to me as we were talking, during a pony race weekend we could set aside an area where we could hold a kinky car boot sale."

"Selling what?" Bert asked.

"I'm sure there are many who have bondage toys etcetera they no longer use and costumes that are not in favour anymore. Some craftsmen may have torture furniture they might want to try and sell to the public."

"Yes, I can see the potential," Bery agreed. "We will need to write in the licence that they must clear up all rubbish at the end of the event. If not, we might be left disposing of a field of rubbish and it will take away any profit we make."

Chapter Nine

The good thing about our future finances is we now have enough sissies to hold two classes and some sissies have signed up for the advanced course. Mistress Viki was holding our first advanced course. I went along to see how she was doing. Of course, all the sissies attending were already known to us and were familiar faces. Mistress Viki clapped her hands to bring the new class to attention.

"I'm glad you have all got to class nice and early that's a good start. You girls have decided to stay for the advanced sissy maid course. This morning we are going to split into groups of two and you're going demonstrate your chambermaid skills. We have six live-in Mistresses who are loath to tidy their own rooms and you lucky girls are going to change their bed linen and clean their rooms for them. Any questions?"

"Who will check our work?" asked a sissy at the back of the class.

"I'll check your work, all the Mistresses are busy working elsewhere in the manor. I will come along after you with my tickling stick and ensure you have cleaned the rooms to the highest standards. Before we leave for the guest rooms can anyone tell me what a chambermaid needs to do in each room?" A great many hands went up, and Mistress chose one at the back of the room.

"Make the beds up with fresh linen, empty rubbish baskets, clean the floor, window sills and dust, including the skirting boards," the sissy replied confidently she had got it right.

"Good girl," Mistress said with a congratulatory clap of her hand. "That's right, not forgetting to wipe down the windows and polish mirrors, and how long should take two girls to clean one room?" Mistress asked.

The same sissy puts her hand up, but Mistress dismissed it, "no we'll try someone else this time. You," Mistress Viki said, pointing to a tall, slender sissy at the front.

"Fifteen minutes," the girl hesitantly replied.

"Yes, that's about right, it shouldn't take any longer than fifteen minutes per room. I will allow a little bit longer today as most of you will not have done such work before, I will however, expect the highest standard of work from each of you. Right sissies, pair off into twos and we will go up to the first floor and get you started."

The sissies followed Mistress up to the first floor, I flowed discreetly behind the entourage.

When everyone arrived on the first floor Mistress went over to a large cupboard.

" In this cupboard, you'll find all the fresh linen you'll need plus cleaning equipment. Each floor has a similar cupboard to this one. Therefore, there is no need to take cleaning materials or linen from one floor to the next. Each cupboard is replenished once a week by our staff."

"There are only Mistresses rooms on this floor so I shall leave you to get started, I'll be back to check on your work in thirty minutes, so stay in the room when you have finished cleaning and wait for my return," Mistress said leaving the girls to select the linen and cleaning materials they needed and get cleaning.

Mistress Viki and I went back downstairs to the kitchen to make a cup of tea and enjoy a biscuit. When we returned the sissies curtseyed and stood to attention in each of the rooms waiting to be inspected. Mistress Viki had her tickling stick with her and was expected to be using it, she wasn't disappointed.

Mistress entered the first room and ignored the sissies who curtseyed and then stood rigidly to attention while Mistress marched around the room checking that the sheets were folded properly at the corners and rubbing her finger over any dust, followed by a murmur of disapproval. Then she went up to a wardrobe which was light and on casters and pulled it forward.

"Come here girls," Mistress bellowed. The girls stepped forward, terrified at what Mistress had found. "What am I looking at?" Mistress asked, pointing at the floor behind the wardrobe.

"Dust," croaked a sissy.

"That's right dust, why is there dust?" the sissies failed to answer, "I can tell you why there is dust, you haven't moved any of the furniture you have just vacuumed and dusted around it. Come to the bed and stand side by side." The girls did as they were told.

"Now removed your panties and tights, pull up your skirts and bend over the bed. Moments later two pink bare bottoms presented themselves almost touching side by side for the attention of the Mistress's tickling stick. The two girls cried out so loudly as Mistress caned one and then the other in turn. It must have terrified the sissies who were still waiting to be inspected as they could no doubt hear what was going on. Mistress Viki went from room to room and did the same thing pulling out the wardrobe with exactly the same results. Each sissy got the same treatment from the tickling stick.

Mistress Viki seemed quite pleased with watching out every sissy which required ample use of her cane.

"I enjoyed that," Mistress said to me as we went downstairs. "I just knew not one girl would think of moving the furniture."

"They got their just rewards," I said in acknowledgement.

"Oh yes, Mistress agreed they need to learn."

In the afternoon lesson, when the sissies returned to class they were greeted with ironing boards instead of desks and at the side of the ironing boards was a basket full to the brim with freshly washed linen.

"I don't need to explain what this afternoon lesson is all about, you can see for yourselves," Mistress announced. "Ironing is a major role for a sissy and every sissy maid can expect to iron for their Mistresses. On the floor at the side of the ironing board is a basket full of bed linen fo you to iron to the highest standard. Unfortunately, there isn't enough ordinary ironing for you all to do, so you're let off lightl with just sheets, tea clothes and bed sheets. So should be an easy task for all of you. If any of you fail this simple task watch out," Mistress concluded, leaving the room and the girls to their tasks.

On the second day, I rejoined the advanced clas to see what Mistress Viki had installed for the sissy's today.

"Attention, attention," Mistress Viki bellowed to a noisy class. "Listen up all you sissies must take an early lunch today because at 1 pm you'l be serving Matron and I and the other Mistresses lunch in the Great Hall. Waitressing is a major role of the average sissy maid and it needs to be done properly," Mistress paused for the information to sink into the sissies' minds.

"Right, has any of you girls heard the term Silver Service?" Mistress asked, surprised that not a single sissy had heard of it before. "Well, it is for the want of a better description of a formal way of serving guests food and drinks. I shall now explain what Silver Service is and at lunchtime, you lucky girls can put your newfound skills into practice." Mistress sat back down at her desk and opened a manual and began to recite:

"Sissy waitresses must adhere to the correct etiquette. This guide aims to teach you the basics of silver service etiquette."

"We will start with a little history for you sissies. Silver Service has been around for hundreds of years. But unless you've eaten at high-end restaurants, or stayed in the best hotels, you may not have heard of or experienced silver service before."

"Silver service started in the 17th and 18th centuries. The waitress would walk around the table, serving the guests from her platter directly onto their plates. This particular service style is called 'Silver Service'. And it was very popular in high-end restaurants and 5-star hotels up to the modern day. These skills are vital for the average sissy to learn."

"Silver service is a method of food service that's performed from the left side. The guest to the host or principal is served first. The service continues clockwise so the staff doesn't bump into each other whilst serving. Plates and glasses are cleared from the right. Glasses are stacked in a line to the right. With wine served in order by course and water glasses in front."

"Silver service tends to be easier for a right-handed waitress. You stand behind the guest to their left side. Holding and supporting the silverware with your left hand and serving the food with your right hand. This requires a great deal of practice and dexterity. You girls should practice whenever you can to keep these skills refreshed. Any questions girls?" Mistress asked. The sissies looked confused and unsure of themselves. "Then I'll continue."

"Plates are served from the left and cleared from the right side. This makes the guests feel less enclosed. Use your right hand to clear a used plate, and your left hand to slide in a fresh plate. The only exception to this is if there is an object on the right side, such as a glass or if the guest is obstructing the way physically (perhaps leaning across the table). In this case, do not lean across the guest, and simply remove plates from the left side."

"Glasses should remain on the table throughout the entire meal, as guests will have their own preferences for the beverages they drink. You may remove any sherry glasses. If a guest asks for glasses to be removed then you should always do so. Always change the wine glass when a guest asks for a new type of wine."

"Present sweets, chocolates, or glazed fruits in compotes. When clearing the table you must keep the noise down. Never ever stack several plates or clear on a tray. Carry each plate individually to the kitchen."

"Before pudding, everything must be cleared from the table that isn't relevant to the final courses. Start with the largest item and work down to the smallest. To speed this process up you can use a small doily-lined tray. As this will prevent slippage and reduce noise."

Clearing crumbs from the table is key to freshening up before pudding. Stand to the left of each guest. Then, with a thin brush or folded napkin, brush the crumbs onto a small plate or tray held just below the edge of the table."

Now, that was easy to absorb, wasn't it girls? I shall pass out to you a printout of what I have just read out, so between now and lunchtime you can sit quietly and read the Silver Service rules and procedures over and over until you understand them because at lunchtime you'll be on your own and remember Matron and I will be watching you closely for errors. Now before I get sissy Susan to pass you each a printout, are there any more questions. This is your last chance lunchtime you're doing Silver Service for real and I will add every day until the end of the week as this is a vital part of your training and will hold you in good stead for the future." Mistress said in conclusion before handing a

pile of printouts to Susan for distribution to eac
sissy.

Chapter Ten

The proposed Pony Race turned into something
much grander and it became an Open Day for
all. Not only were there to be pony races, but w
also laid on a car boot sale for all that is kinky.
In addition to this, we set aside an area in the
foyer for a small café to serve cold drinks,
snacks and beverages to thirsty visitors. We also
put some torture furniture outside on the
grounds for customers to use at their leisure.
There were also a K9 element and human dogs
would be made to perform in a Cruft's dog
show. The garden was adorned with several
marquees including a thriving beer tent.

When the open day arrived the gods were with us it was the last flood of summer and it was a gorgeous day with temperatures in the mid-seventies and wall-to-wall sunshine. All our guestrooms were booked solid so much so we had to rope in the beginner's sissy class to help out as chambermaids.

We seemed to cater for every kink known to mankind, and we also had some commercial interest, a cosmetic company that held a store and gave out free samples to passing sissies and Mistresses. It was a happy jolly day good-natured and fun, and what's more, it added need funds to our coffers.

It got so hot in the afternoon we opened up the outdoor pool for guests to cool off. I watched the last pony race of the day. This event was very popular and the ponies were generally young nubile women raced by their Masters, who sat in purpose-made chariots with their dressage whips.

In the evening we all moved indoors as it was now autumn and the temperatures soon dipped once the sun began to set. I had invited my own personal sissy maid Isabel to join us for the weekend. I thought it would be a treat for her as she was all on her own at our house in Surrey, keeping it clean for our occasional return.

I dressed her in a frilly frock with lashings of lace and bows which she seemed to like. I always thought it strange, sissies long to be women, yet the average lady wouldn't be seen dead in such ultra-feminine clothes. I suppose they're making up for years of lost time dressed as a male. However, Isabel loved her frock and I finished it off with a dog collar and long chain which I put over my shoulder and dragged the poor girl around with me as I mingled with the paying guests. I wanted everybody to see I had my own cherished slave in tow. I could hear poor Isabel trip and stumble behind me trying to keep up, but I took no notice of her remonstrations.

We stopped to watch a nubile young woman in her twenties being whipped by her Master with a riding crop on the St Andrews Cross. The Master a much older man in his early fifties laid into the girl and she took each cruel stroke without so much as a murmur. She had been on the cross for some time as her back, shoulders and buttocks were covered in angry red welts, yet she continued to take her punishment without as much as a whimper.

When the hapless girl was released from the cross there seemed to be no takers and the little gathering began to disperse.

"Isabel," I said making the girl jump with the suddenness of my voice. "You haven't had any punishment for weeks now, I think it is time to remedy this, go up to the cross please," I said pointing to the contraption. Poor Isabel reluctantly stepped up to the cross. This caught the attention of the dispersing crowd and most returned to see my maid get her punishment.

"Take your frock off," I ordered, "and fold it neatly and put it on the nearby chair. Now step up to the cross with your front to the device." I stepped up behind her and began to restrain the girl tying her spread-eagled to the cross. Once she was trusted to the device. I span it so she could enjoy going upside down a couple of times before it clicked to a halt. Then I went off to the whip rack to choose my implement. There was a lovely dressage whip, I decided to choose that as it would make a lot of noise and would look dramatic for the assembling audience.

made a few practice strokes in the thin air to get poor Isabel cringing with anticipation for what was to come. I felt so powerful to have such total control over another human being that felt ten feet tall, I also relished having an excited audience to watch me perform. I went up and whispered into Isabel's ear as I massaged her back and bottom.

This is going to hurt you more than me," I said mockingly. Then I stood back and cracked the thin whip on her flank and watched a thin white line appear, which soon turned red and swollen. Isabel took the first stoke without a sound.

"The first of many," I said, laying on another stroke on the buttocks this time. This stroke had Isabel pulling on her restraints. After about six or seven strokes, Isabel gave me ample feedback as she wriggled, cried and begged me to stop. I knew what punishment she was capable of taking and took no notice of her pleas and continued to lay on the whip. After about twenty strokes I decided to stop and as I was about to untie Isabel the audience seem to think I had stopped too early and encouraged me to continue whipping.

So to please the audience, I gave poor Isabel another dozen or so strokes which gained the approval of the gathering. Then, when Isabel was crying, weeping heap I untied her and she dressed I attached her chain again and took her off as she rubbed her wounds into the crowd.

When I released Isabel I put the chain back on her collar and went off to see what else was going on. We entered a room with a line of chairs against each wall. On half of these chairs sat a hapless female naked from the waist down with their legs spread wide and fastened to the chair legs. Their Master or Mistress was busy applying weights and clamps to their genitals. One Master was busy whipping off clamps with the tip of his riding crop and the poor slave wriggling in unbelievable pain. Most of the girls had swollen eyes and had clearly been crying from the attention of their owners.

I decided to leave the ladies to their fate and Isabel and I found a vacant table in our makeshift café. I had Isabel kneel at my side as I ordered us both a cold drink. I noticed just before our drinks arrived Isabel had a particularly angry welt that had become very swollen on her thigh. When a sissy waitress put our drinks down on the table I took a lump of ice from one of the glasses and rubbed it on Isabel's welts. This had her jumping more than she did on the cross.

"Don't be such a sissy," I said mockingly. "It will help to bring down the swelling." Did you enjoy your whipping?" I asked as I applied the ice.

"No," Isabel said, pouting. She never admitted to enjoying being punished, but clearly Isabel did like chastisement or she would have stopped visiting me long ago.

"I am sure you did, you relished all the attention," I replied mockingly.

I decided to be kind to Isabel and removed her collar and told her to go off and enjoy herself. I said if I needed her I'll come and find her, but I was content to let her finish the day doing whatever she wanted. I even told her to put her drinks from the beer tent on my slate. Once Isabel shot off into the milling crowd Bert came up and took her warmed seat at the coffee table. Bert looked concerned and a bit worried.

"What's on your mind?" I asked, "if you ask me today is a raging success and we will make a mint in takings."

"Yes, I agree the day has worked out very well," Bert replied.

"Then," I asked, "what is troubling you?" I asked.

"It might just be my imagination, but some of our visitors may not be what they seem," Bert said as he ordered a coffee from a waiting sissy waitress.

"What do you mean?" I asked.

"Do you see on the far side of the foyer, two men leaning against the wall talking to each other?" Bert asked. I looked in the direction in which Bert pointed.

"Yes, I see them, so what?" I asked becoming slightly concerned.

"I have been watching them for some time. What brought them to my attention is they are not like our other guests, they stick out like sore thumbs." Bert said.

"Surely you're just imagining things," I replied reassuringly.

"I also noticed they haven't engaged in any activity or spoken to any of the guests, they have kept to themselves and have observed everything that is going on here today. Almost everybody here is in a dominant-submissive relationship. Even if they are gay, they don't take me as a dominant-submissive couple, after years in the scene I can tell who is into the scene and who isn't. These two men aren't scene players." Bert concluded.

"Then," I replied who do you think they are?"

"I don't know police, council officials, who knows, but I have a bad feeling about them. I ust can't shake them from my mind," Bert replied looking very serious. Well, even if Bert was right, there was nothing we could do so we decided to forget it and worry when we had something to worry about.

Bert finished his coffee and went back off into the crowd and I continued to mingle with the guests. My dear friend Mistress Christine held a stall where she was selling an assortment of different violet wands. She had brought her slave along to demonstrate the different devices. When I arrived at her stall she was demonstrating to the crowd a thing which looked suspiciously like a cattle prod, which she poked at her hapless slave which had him reeling in pain and doubling over to the excitement of those who watched. When there was a lull in the activity I asked her:

"Have you sold many violet wands, Christine?"

"Oh yes, six so far, that has paid for my stall, fuel here and a nice little profit to take home. I would imagine you have done well today too?" Mistress Christine suggested.

"Yes," I replied. The money we make today is much needed for us to stay afloat," just as I finished speaking, I saw out of the corner of my eye the two mysterious men Bert referred to come into the room.

"Christine," I asked. "See those two men do you know either of them?" I asked.

"I don't think so," Mistress Christine replied. "They don't look familiar to me," she added as she examined the men more closely.

"I think I know one of them," said Mistress Christine's slave as he came over to us.

. "Go on," I asked what can you tell me about him?" I asked.

"I think I have seen the taller one before at the council building when I applied for housing benefits," he said.

"Robin lives close by," Mistress Christine said qualifying Robin's remarks.

"Are you sure?" I asked.

"I can't be too sure I have only seen him the once I might be mistaken," Robin the slave said, shaking his head as if he wasn't too sure of himself.

"How sure are you out of 1 to 10?" I asked.

"Maybe a 7," he replied, "but I don't want to worry you, I might still be mistaken."

I thanked Mistress Christine's slave and we chatted some more and I went back into the masses. I decided not to worry Bert with my discoveries as Robin wasn't that sure of himself, although his suspicions certainly fitted in with what Bert feared. However, there was no point in worrying about the unknown. We were doing nothing illegal and everything we were doing was well within the manor grounds and out of sight of the general public.

The last activity I observed that day was the school class, held in classroom number one. Except it wasn't used for sissy training instead for just one day it was a mathematics class for those who liked to behave like schoolboys. This was held by Mistress Fiona, who dressed as a school Mistress for the occasion. She donned black a pencil skirt, a white frilly blouse which emphasised her voluptuous breasts, and large-rimmed secretary glasses, rounded off with a black university-type gown. Her pupils too required to be dressed as schoolboys in short grey trousers and blue blazers.

Mistress Fiona would scribble a really difficult equation on the blackboard and ask a hapless pupil to solve the sum. Odds on, of course, he would get the answer wrong and would be called to the front of the class for punishment. The errant boy would be made to come to the head of the class to bare his bottom and bend over a chair for Mistress Fiona to decide how many strokes of a dragon school cane he should receive for his errors.

Mistress Fiona seemed in her element and thoroughly enjoying herself as a teacher, so I left her to her class and went back behind the scene to have a rest and give Bert a bit of company.

Chapter Eleven

A short while after the open day Bert had completed the accounts and announced a healthy profit, so we did some market research and decided to have a similar event once a month. For the first time, it looked as if our business will survive and the future was being to look rosy. The sissy maid classes were doing well and we had garnered a good reputation with high-end Mistresses who wanted the best quality servants. We now had four classes and had to hire more Mistresses to serve in the Torture Room where we were now shorthanded because we had also added a nursery for adult babies and we needed wet nurses as a temporary measure used Mistresses from the Torture Room.

We also had some stables built to house pony-racing chariots as some had been damaged by the rain. In addition, we discreetly had a race circuit made which would blend in with the manicured gardens without looking out of place. Bert improved our website and we had flyers made to distribute at fetish venues across the country. We were rapidly becoming a well-established organisation within our community.

On the next open day which was an equal success financially to the first open event. However, we did encounter a problem which confirmed one of Bert's fears. One of our guests arrived late. I heard their car screech up to the front door as it chewed up the loose gravel. In ran a puffed-out couple. The man was so excited he could hardly speak, so his wife took over and said.

"About a mile back," she said animatedly, "we saw a convoy of police vehicles parked up, we think you're about to be raided." I didn't wait for further explanation and went directly to the personal address system and announced over the

speaker which sounded both inside and outsid
in the grounds.

"Attention everybody, this is urgent, please sto
what you are doing and listen. We believe we'r
about to be raided by the police. Can you a
please help to remove anything B.D.S.M
related to the storage sheds, which will b
shown to you by the servants. No time to waste
Also if anyone of our guests is usin;
recreational drugs, which I might add is agains
our rules, I suggest you dispose of then
immediately."

I was pleasantly surprised everyone became
galvanised and wasted no time in clearing up th
manor of incriminating objects. Although
should add we were in fact doing nothing
illegal; that doesn't account for society's
prejudices. Fifteen minutes later as expected a

convoy of police vehicles with flashing blue lights descended on us in droves.

One of the men we were suspicious of at the earlier open day came up to us with a smug look on his face and passed Bert a search warrant, and suggested he had complaints of fornication and drug taking. I got angry and said.

"I remember you, you were here at the last open day, and you saw for yourself there was nothing illegal taking place, everything you saw was legal and consensual, and you're just a bigot."

The man took no notice of my remonstrations and began to order his entourage and the police began to search the premises. After a couple of hours of disruption to our routine, the police left empty-handed and neither Bert, the guests and I were charged with anything.

We thought that might be the end of matters and we continued as usual with the greatest focus on sissy training which was our bread and butter and provided the lion's share of our income.

One morning I came down the grand staircase with the intention of sitting in on one of Mistress Viki's classes. When I noticed at each end of the foyer stood two sissy maids with their faces to the wall and their hands on their heads. They both stood there rigid and as quiet as mice. I assumed they were under punishment and thought no more of it, However, late afternoon I noticed the two sissy maids were still there as they were first thing in the morning. Neither sissy seemed to have moved an inch.

I rejoined Mistress Viki's class which she was winding up for the day. When the classroom cleared of sissies I spoke to Mistress Viki and asked.

"Have you forgotten about the two sissies in the foyer?"

"No," Mistress Viki replied forcefully, "they have both been caned and given some time out. When I arrived in class this morning the two girls were fighting. I will not have fights in my class. Each girl got given eighteen of the cane in front of the class, but I thought that wasn't sufficient punishment and also gave them time out," Mistress Viki said demonstrating how seriously she took her classes."

"Well," I said, "they have been standing looking at the wall all day, I should waste no time dismissing them or they will be peeing on the nicely polished floor." Mistress Viki smiled mischievously and went to the classroom door and bellowed.

"You two errant sissies are dismissed to go straight to the bathroom and then to the food hall and tomorrow, let's have no fighting in my class if you know what's good for you."

Some of our most well trained sissies were privileged to serve us in our communal restroom for Mistresses. We usually chose two different sissies each evening and they would be stationed on each side of the restroom door and demurely wait until one of the Mistresses required their services. The idea was to give the sissies, real-time service so they would know what to expect when they finally find their own Mistress to serve. They also had to endure physical punishment if their standards weren't of the highest quality. This gave some sissies the chance to put into practice all the skills they learnt in class, including curtseying and feminine deportment.

When I came into the restroom one evening such a punishment was taking place. One sissy forgot to curtsey when she left the room and was called over by one of the Mistresses, which tore a strip off the sissy and made her stand on ne table and pull up her skirt and lower her nickers for all present to see. The girl stood on ne table quivering whilst Mistress went off to ind her favourite cane. Some moments later Mistress returned swishing the cane, which the ound made the sissy almost fall off the table vith anticipation of what was to come.

Touch your toes," The Mistress bellowed at the op of her voice. The other Mistresses in the oom turned their seats to watch the spectacle. The hapless sissy did as she was told and bent over to touch her toes. The poor girl quivered as she waited for the inevitable. Mistress took her ime and placed the cane on the sissy's bare bottom and let it stay there for several agonising seconds before she pulled it back and laid on the first stroke which had the errant sissy scream out and almost fall off the table.

"You really are a sissy, aren't you," Mistress mocked. "That was only the first stroke yo have plenty more to come my girl, so get a gri and hold your ankles tight." The girl did tak twelve hard strokes before she was allowed t return to the door and stand with the other sissy She rubbed her sore pained bottom furiously a she went back to her station.

I took a seat and ordered a coffee. I had brough a magazine to read but was distracted by th discipline that was meted out to the two servin sissies. Now it was the turn of the other sissy t get chastised. The poor girl was hectored and bullied so much by the Mistresses present, she ended up dropping a tray of hot coffee on the floor. To add to her crime one Mistress got he arm splashed. I don't think she was hurt very much, but it gave her the excuse to punish the girl, first though she was sent away to find cloths to clear up the mess she created. The girl returned with her tail between her legs and began to mop away the mess. When she had finished cleaning up to the satisfaction of the offended Mistress she was told to strip off to her bra and panties.

While the sissy was undressing the Mistress went off to fetch something and she returned to the semi-naked sissy who looked very frightened.

"You may now take your knickers off and stand here in the centre of the room for all to see," Mistress said in an authoritative and commanding voice. She was bent over and given liberal strokes of the riding crop until her bottom was covered in welts but her punishment didn't end there. She was now told to open her feet as wide as possible. When the sissy had done as told. Mistress knelt and attached a lighted lantern on a chain to the sissies scrotum by a crocodile clip.

"You will stand there until the candle in the lantern goes out," Mistress said. After some minutes the sissy cried out she was getting too hot and the lantern was beginning to burn.

"Too bad the candle is only half burnt away, you'll stay there until it goes out," Mistress said without any sign of mercy.

"You need to swirl the lantern with your hips to disperse the heat," said a kinder Mistress giving the tortured maid a demonstration by wiggling her hips to show the clueless sissy what to do. It was quite a sight watching the sissy maid swirl away until finally, the candle went out with a final puff of smoke. The affronted Mistress smiled and come over and pulled off the lantern with a final yelp of the sissy as the clamp tore at the sissy's balls before coming away.

"You may put your clothes back on and take your place by the door," Mistress said, returning to her seat with her smoke-stained lantern.

Chapter Twelve

Over the next few weeks, everything went well. Our sissy classes were full including the advanced classes. The Torture Room was booked up too. The nursery had some takers, but this was less popular than other B.D.S.M., activities, nevertheless, it brought in much-needed revenue.

However, our bubble was about to burst. One snowy morning we had a visit by the local council officials. They spoke to Bert and me in our office and then with us in tow inspected the house and grounds, after we returned to the office to hear their finding and verdict on what they saw. Apparently, we did not meet the fire regulations and were given a long list of what was needed to remedy the problems. Then they turned to the kitchens which also didn't meet council approval and were given yet another long list of repairs and changes that needed doing. The real shock was we were only given one month to make the changes or we will be closed down permanently.

After the council officials went on, Bert bowed his head and said to me in a very serious voice:

"I'll price up the repairs and changes demanded by the council, but I fear we won't be able to afford it," he said dejectedly.

Just as we were reeling from the council visit, we had another unwanted visit the same day, another council official from a different office and department arrived. He told us he had received complaints from people living locally about traffic congestion, loud music coming from our grounds and lurid behaviour. It was then we realised this was a concerted effort by officials to have us closed down by hook or crook. This time the council official said before leaving if he receives further complaints he will be forced to close us down immediately without notice. This left us with a dilemma was it worth going to great expense to have the repair work done by the first lot of officials if we were going to get closed down anyway by the second official? Before we knee-jerked into a position, Bert went to work on pricing up the repair work that needed doing. Later that afternoon he called me into the office.

'I have very bad news for you, Bridget," Bert said solemnly. "Do you want it from the hip, or sugarcoated?"

"Sugarcoated," I replied in jest.

"Okay," we can't afford the repairs, it will put us into too much debt to recover," Bert said awaiting my response.

"Now from the hip," I replied.

"We're going to have to close down. Even if w dropped the B.D.S.M., activities and started a more orthodox business, we would still not be able to pay for the repairs."

"What do we do?" I asked Bert.

"For the time being we just keep going as we are and make as much money as we can until we're forced to stop." We did as Bert suggested except we didn't take on any new clients just those that had already booked.

In the meantime, I had a long chat on the phone with my friend Mistress Christine and told her our bad news. Christine was quite upset upon hearing about our misfortune. Christine was a good shoulder for me to lean on and we chatted for over an hour trying to think of a way out of our predicament. Before she rang off she said she would call me if she thought of any more ideas.

I suppose two weeks went by after I chatted with Christine. Since my telephone call with Christine, we have received a letter from the council forcing us to close without further notice. Bert had already started to sell the torture furniture and had the grounds cleared of anything fetish related. The manor seemed so empty now there were no sissies, slaves and Mistresses coming and going. The house wasn't the same anymore, it seemed cold, quiet and uninviting.

It was the end and just when we were doing so well. Even Bert, who was never enthusiastic about the enterprise was depressed and saddened that it all had to come to an end. The only saving grace was the house was now worth five times what we had paid for it which eased the pain, but it didn't compensate for the time and effort we put into the business which was a success and only failed because of society's prejudices.

We had no problem selling Windrush Manor and on the last day, we sat on the lawn and drank red wine and reminisced about all the good times and trials and errors we experienced. We were getting quite tipsy and morbid when Isabel my maid came rushing over panting.

"There's a telephone call for you Mistress Bridget," she said with urgency.

"Who's calling?" I asked.

"Mistress Christine I think, she says it is important she chats with you."

"I had better go and take the call," I said to Bert as I stood and followed Isabel into the building.

"I'm glad I got you," said Christine down the phone. "I thought as it is your last day you might be too busy to speak to me."

"What is so important?" I asked.

"Have you sold the manor?" She asked.

"Yes, we have and made a handsome profit, we will exchange contracts tomorrow," I replied wondering what Christine would say next.

"Have you ever been to Portugal?" she asked mysteriously.

"Portugal," I repeated, "why Portugal, and no I have never been?"

"I am here in Portugal as I speak and I want you to come out next weekend if you can make it," Christine pleaded.

"As you might imagine we're very busy at the moment," I replied as I wasn't too keen on the idea of taking time off so soon when we still have so much to sort out.

"It will be to your advantage I promise you, I can't say too much on the phone, please say you'll come." Christine pleaded.

At that moment Bert came into the room and before Christine hung up, I asked him if he could spare me for a long weekend.

"I'll manage," Bert replied. "I can stay here and sort out what needs to be done, you go and have a short break it will do you good."

I took Bert at his word and on Friday evening I was standing in the queue having my passport checked at Stanstead Airport. It was mid-winter in England with snow on the ground, but in Portugal, it was the first flood of spring and I relished in the warm air as I waited outside Faro airport waiting for Christine to arrive. I saw a little car pull up and could see Christine's smiling face behind the wheel. I struggled over with my cases. Christine got out of the car to help me put the luggage in the boot.

"I'm so glad you could make it, you won't be disappointed," she said opening the passenger door for me. We drove for around an hour, then we turned off the main beating track and took an unmade road until we arrived at a farm by a wide river.

"We're here," Christine announced. A late middle-aged couple heard us arrive and stood at the farm gate to greet us.

"Welcome to the La Mariposa," said the ginger-haired man putting out his hand for a shake. The lady of the house also gave me a welcome hug and we followed them to the farmhouse door.

Christine and I sat at a large oak table in a very big country kitchen. In moments we were serve a very welcome homemade lemonade and ice. Our hosts joined us at the table,

"My name is Frank and my wife's name is Jacklin. Has Christine told you very much abou why we are asking you here today?" He asked with curiosity.

"Not very much at all," I said, "except coming here today was to my advantage," I replied.

"Come with us, bring your lemon aid with you, seeing is better than describing," the man said somewhat mysteriously. Christine and I followed the couple outside into the warm sunshine and walked down towards the river.

"Oh look," I said to Christine, I can see wooden stocks, this reminds me of the manor."

"Look over there," Frank said, "there is a slave tied to the trees getting a strapping from his Mistress." We followed the couple down to the river bank where we saw a ducking stool just like the one they used for errant, nagging wives in the middle ages.

"For wives who talk too much," Frank explained, "just like in the olden days, it is our most popular torture device. It is usually in great demand and regularly used by our clients."

"It appears as if this is a very similar operation to what we had in the UK?" I said glancing at all that was going on.

Yes, Jacklin replied. The big difference is we have been in business for eight years plus without any interference from officialdom."

"Are the authorities here more open-minded?" I asked.

"No, they are probably more bigoted than in the UK, the big difference is we are miles from anywhere, and no one knows what we get up to. Our nearest neighbour is two miles away. Because we are a farm we don't pay council tax and we are almost self-sufficient. Therefore, we don't need to rub shoulders with officialdom or the locals very much and they are probably not aware we are here."

"I am so envious of you, just as we were succeeding when we were forced to close down," I replied.

"Yes, I know," Frank replied, "Christine, has told us everything. Let's go back to the house I have something to discuss with you," he said, turning around to walk back to the building. On the way back, I observed a Mistress pulling her male slave along on his hands and knees.

"They're off for their daily walk along the riverbank," Jacklin said, "they are regulars and book a two weeks holiday with us every year and have done so for the last five years."

When we arrived back some sissy maids served us dinner at the big oak table. We were served roast chicken and all the trimmings.

"The chicken is from the farm and fed on corn, you'll taste the difference," Jacklin advised me, "it is much nicer than supermarket chicken. We produce nearly all our own produce."

After dinner and a dessert of chocolate fudge, we retired to the lounge where there was a roaring open fire, as it is only spring and the nights are still cold, we were told. Once settled in big armchairs we were given large brandies which were all very pleasant and I started to feel sleepy and very relaxed.

"I'll come to the point," Frank said dramatically as he took an ample gulp of brandy. "Jacklin and I are getting on a bit and we have enjoyed our time on the farm, but we have agreed it was time to sell and take it easy for what time is left to us. The business takes too much of our attention these days and the enterprise needs new blood, would you be interested? I can show you the books before you go and you'll see we enjoy a healthy profit. Dominants, submissives and couples will pay to come out and visit us for a holiday so they can play in a safe environment and do all the other things one does whilst on holiday."

"Do you get many locals to come up to the farm?" I asked.

"No, not many locals come here. Local B.D.S.M., enthusiasts exist, but they are few and very hardcore," Frank said.

I think it is a good thing," interrupted Jacklin, "as we mainly cater to ex-pats there is even less likelihood of the authorities taking an interest in us if we avoid attracting local interest."

We have spent eight years plus building the business up and we would very much like La Mariposa to continue catering for the fetish community. Dominants and submissives need a holiday in a safe and welcoming environment. We thought you and your husband would be an ideal couple to take over the business, having experience of running something along the same lines," Frank added.

'Yes," Jacklin continued, " we won't be asking for a fortune for the farm or the inventory. If you're prepared to carry on as we have, we'll give you and your husband a handsome discount. It isn't profit we are after but saving the business for the future. We are very keen to sell the farm as a going concern to a like-minded couple, that's our wish."

This seemed like a dream come true to carry on with the sissy academy and other B.D.S.M., activities without fear of being closed down. There were also other bonuses a river and wall-to-wall sunshine and long summers. It would be a good place for Bert and me to retire and take it easy, all I had to do was sell the idea to him. It would be a harder sell than the manor, with us having been forced to close down. I had to bring him out to Portugal to speak to Frank himself and see the setup.

It was a hard sell, but with the usual moaning and cajoling, I got Bert to see my point of view and eventually we purchased La Mariposa and had ample funds left to weather any financial crisis the future may bestow on us. Many of our regular sissies came out to join us, including

Isabel, who came out to serve us permanently. It wasn't long before we established another thriving business based on pampering like-minded people in our community.

The End.

Check out my other books:

The Chronicles of a Male Slave.

A real-life account of a consensual slave. The book follows the life of an individual who comes to terms with his submissive side and his search for a Mistress and his subsequent experiences as a consensual slave.
This book gives a real insight into the B.D.S.M., lifestyle and what it is like to be a real slave to a lifestyle Mistress.

Mistress Margaret.

This is the story of young teenage Brenden, who is finding out about his sexuality when he meets older Mistress Margaret a nonprofessional dominatrix. Mistress Margaret takes Brenden's hand and shows him the mysterious, erotic world of BDSM and all it has to offer.

The Week That Changed My Life.

A tale about a young girl discovering her sexuality with an older, more mature dominant man whilst on a week's holiday by the sea. She was introduced into a world of BDSM that would change her outlook on life forever.

The Temple of Gor.

Hidden in the wilds of Scotland is The Temple of Gor, a secret BDSM society. In the Temple, you will find Masters and their female slaves living in a shared commune. The community is based on the Gorean subculture depicted in a fictional novel by John Norman and has taken a step too far and turned into a macabre reality. Stella a young girl from England, stumbles on the commune and is captured and turned into a Kajira slave girl until she finds a way to escape her captors.

Becoming a Sissy Maid.

This is a true story of one person's quest to become a sissy maid for a dominant couple. The story outlines the correspondence between the Master, Mistress, and sissy maid, that leads up to their first and second real-time meeting.

It is a fascinating tale and is a true, honest and accurate account, only the names and places have been changed to protect the individuals involved. It is a must-be-read book by anyone into BDSM and will give an interesting insight for anyone wishing to become in the future a real-time sissy maid.

Meet Maisy The Sissy Maid.

This story is about Maisy a sissy maid and her life. The story takes Maisy through all the various stages a sissy has to make take to find her true submissive and feminine self. It is a long and arduous road and many transitions before Maisy finds true happiness as a lady's maid for her Mistress.

Beginner's Guide For The Serious Sissy

So you want to be a woman and dress and behave like a sissy? You accept you cannot compete with most men and now want to try something new and different. This guide will help you along the way and walk the potential sissy through the advantages and pitfalls of living as a submissive woman.

Becoming a serious sissy requires making changes that are both physical and mental. This will involve learning to cross-dress, leg-crossing, sit, stand, bend hair removal, wear makeup, use cosmetics, and sit down to pee.

You'll learn feminine mannerisms such as stepping daintily, arching your spine, swishing your hips, and adopting a feminine voice. You'll understand more about hormone treatment and herbal supplements.

There is advice and tips on going out in public for the first time and coming out of the closet to friends, colleagues, and family. The guide will give help you to slowly lose your masculine identity and replace it with a softer gentle feminine one.

A Collaring For A Sissy.

Collaring ceremonies are taken very seriously by the BDSM community and are tantamount to a traditional wedding. Lots of thought and planning go into such an event and can take many forms.

Mistress Anastasia's sissy maid Paula has just completed her six months probation and has earned her collar. This is a story about Paula's service and her subsequent collaring ceremony.

The Secret Society.

Rene Glock is a freelance journalist looking for a national scoop and attempts to uncover and expose a Secret Society of Goreans which have set up residence in an old nightclub. However, as he delves into the secret world he finds he has an interest in BDSM and questions his moral right to interfere in what goes on in the Gorean Lodge.

The Good Master and Mistress Guide.

If you want to become a good Dominant and practice BDSM in a safe and considerate way, then this guide is for you.

It is written by a submissive that has had many dominants male and female over the years and knows what goes into becoming a good dominant and the mistakes some dominants make.

The book is not aimed to teach, but to make the fledgling dominant understand what is going on in the dominant-submissive dynamic, so they can understand their charges better and become better dominants.

My Transgender Journey

This is a true story with some minor alterations to protect people's identities. It is a tale about my own journey into transgender and my eventual decision to come out.

It is hoped that others can share my experiences, relate to them and perhaps take comfort from some of them.

The book has some BDSM content but is only used to put my story into context, it's about my experiences, trials and tribulations of coming out and living as a female full-time.

I hope you enjoy my little story.

Cinders

Cinders is the BDSM version of Cinderella. It is a story where an orphaned Tommy is sent to be brought up by his aunt and two very beautiful sisters.

The sisters were cruel and taunting and dressed Tommy up like a Barbie Doll. One day Tommy was caught with Auntie's bra and knickers and as a punishment, he was a feminist and turned into Nancy the maid. Poor Nancy is consigned to a life of drudgery and final acceptance of life as a menial skivvy.

This story doesn't have a glass slipper or a prince, but Nancy is given a present of some new rubber gloves and a bottle of bleach. There is no happy ending or is there, you decide.

At The Races

Ryan is a hotel night porter and is at a crossroads in his life. He feels his talents are being wasted in a job with no future. Through a friend, he is offered a managerial position on a farm in Catalonia, Spain. He decides to take the post but has no idea what sort of farm he is going to work at.

Only on the flight out to Spain does Ryan realise that there is more to the farm than rearing chickens and growing vegetables. Later he learns the main event of the year is The Derby and there isn't a horse in sight.

I Nearly Married A Dominatrix

This is a true story that I have changed a little bit to protect people from identification. It's a story about a man's constant struggle and fights against his deep-rooted need to be submissive and a woman who conversely, is very comfortable with her dominance and heavily into the BDSM lifestyle.

They meet and get along very well indeed until Mistress Fiona announces she wants to become a professional dominatrix. Rex, the submissive boyfriend goes along with his Mistress's plans, reluctantly, but as time goes by there are more and more complications heaped on the relationship until it snaps.

Be careful what you ask for

There is an old English adage: Be careful about what you ask for; it may come true.

This is a story about a BDSM fantasy that has gone badly wrong.

antasy is simply a fantasy and we all have em regardless of our sexuality. Fantasies are uite harmless until we choose to act them out or real and when do act out our fantasies the ine between fantasy and reality can become ery blurred. This is a tale about one person's antasy that becomes all too real for comfort.

etticoat Lane.

 slightly effeminate young boy is taken under he wings of his school teacher. She becomes is guardian and trains him to become a servant irl to serve her for the rest of his life.

An unexpected incident happens and Lucy the naid has an opportunity to escape her life of lrudgery and servitude, but does she take the opportunity or does she stay with her Mistress?

The Life and Times of a Victorian Maid.

This is a story about the life and times of a young Transgender who becomes a Victorian-style maid in a large exclusively B.D.S.M. household. Although fiction this story is largely based on fact, as the author herself lived in such a household for a while as a maid.

It shows the contrast between a place of safety where like-minded people can live in relative harmony and the need for ridged discipline in it serving staff.

There are many thriving households, such as the one mentioned here, tucked away out of sight and away from prying minds.

I Became a Kajira slave girl.

A Gorean scout Simon, who is looking for new talent kidnaps Emma a PhD student on sabbatical with her friend Zoey in Spain. Emma is half-drugged and sent across the ocean to the United States and ends up in the clandestine

City of Gor in the Mojave desert sixty miles from civilization.

Here there is no law women are mere objects for the pleasure of men. Emma becomes a Kajira a female slave whose sole purpose in life is to please her master or be beaten tortured or killed.

Two years into Emma's servitude and she meets Simon again. Simon is consumed with guilt when he sees what Emma has been reduced to, a beaten, downtrodden and abused slave. He vows to free her from her servitude, But how they are in one of the biggest deserts in the world and sixty miles from anywhere?

Training My First Sissy Maid.

A young single mother with a part-time job, two teenage children, and up to her knees in housework is at the end of her tether and finding it harder and harder to cope.

Then reading one of her daughter's kinky magazines she found in her bedroom whilst tidying, read an article about sissy maids who are willing to work without pay just for discipline, control and structure to their lives. Excited about the prospect she decides a maid is an answer to her domestic problems.

She sets about finding a sissy to come and do her housework and be trained and moulded into becoming her loyal obedient sissy maid. On the journey she discovers she is a natural dominant and training her maid becomes a highly erotic and fulfilling experience.

A Week with Mistress Sadistic.

Susan a young female reporter in her thirties wants to know more about B.D.S.M for a future article in her magazine. She arranged to spend a week with Mistress Sadistic and watch how a professional dominatrix works.

After an eye-opening week of watching Mistress Sadistic deal with her many and varied clients, Mistress Sadistic wonders if Susan might be submissive and puts her to the text to make Susan her slave.

Lady Frobisher and her maid Alice.

This is a gripping tale of B.D.S.M., in Victorian England. It is a story about the lives of Lady Frobisher and her hapless maid Alice. It is a tale of lesbianism and sexual sadism with a twist at the end.

If you enjoy reading fetish literature you'll love this as it has everything woven into an interesting tale of two people's lives at the top end of society.

K9

This is a tale that explores an area of B.D.S.M where a Mistress or Master desires a human dog (submissive) to train and treat as a real dog in every respect. Mistress Cruella is one such Mistress who takes on a young male submissive as her human dog and she takes the role of Mistress and her dog very seriously indeed.

Ryan soon becomes Max the Poodle and he struggles with his new role as a pooch but learns to be an obedient dog to please his Mistress. Max soon discovers there is far more to being a dog than meets the eye.

Printed in Great Britain
by Amazon

38243082R00096

In the Footsteps
PILGRI

CW00429800

Keith Sugden

Avebury is a 'superhenge', a prehistoric temple not only older but far larger than Stonehenge. Its sarsen stones were dragged to the site from nearby Fyfield Down; the largest weighs 45 tons.

Pagan Sites

Two of Britain's most evocative and popular shrines are pagan in origin. The Isle of Avalon in Celtic mythology is the mystical land of the dead. For centuries, this paradise has been identified as a magical hill rising out of the Somerset Levels – Glastonbury Tor.

For the Romans and their British subjects, the hot springs of *Aquae Sulis* (modern Bath), unique in Britain, held an even greater attraction. A genuine little shrine-town developed there by the 3rd century AD, now beautifully excavated and explained in the Roman Baths Museum.

The pagan power of Glastonbury Tor, the mystical abode of the dead for the Celts, was neutralised by Christians with a church dedicated to the Archangel Michael.

ABOVE: Supplicants at the Romano-British sacred spring of Aquae Sulis (now called Bath) would sometimes cast curses into the steaming water. Inscribed on lead, they were rolled up to keep their power secret.

The temple of Stonehenge, a shrine of the moon and later of the sun, was a focus for prehistoric religion in Wessex for 1,700 years. Bronze Age chieftains sought to be buried within sight of it.

BELOW: *St Augustine's cross.*

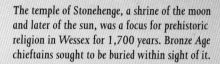

pilgrimage is by no means the sole domain of Christians. Think of the *Hadj* to Mecca, one of the five pillars of Islam; or consider those pagan supplicants at the Delphic Oracle or the great shrine to Aphrodite in Asia Minor. Naturally, ancient philosophy influenced the early Christians. Evangelists generally found it prudent to adapt the pagan beliefs to the new religion rather than simply destroy them, taking on board the old myths and sacred sites. A famous letter from Pope Gregory the Great to St Augustine instructs the 6th-century missionary to build his churches on ancient places of worship. Of course many Britons had been Christians under the Roman Empire, and at a few places in Britain, tradition or modern research claims that Christianity never died out during the pagan invasions of the Dark Ages – Glastonbury in Somerset and Deerhurst in Gloucestershire are among them.

St Augustine and his followers began their mission in England by converting the Saxon royal families; from that point the faith of the individual kings led to the replacement of the pagan beliefs. Some rulers became so devout that their own souls took precedence over the kingdom. Such was King Ina of Wessex, who gave his throne to a kinsman and made the 'permanent pilgrimage' to Rome, founding there the English Hospice in AD727 (which still exists close to the Vatican). Many wealthy Englishmen of the day followed suit, trusting that by dying at Rome, close to the bearer of the keys of heaven, St Peter, they would stand the best possible chance on the Day of Judgement.

RIGHT: *The Gorgon's head from the pediment of the temple in Bath, found in 1790 when the Pump Room was being built, also represents Sul, god of the sacred spring.*

✠ Motives & Means

In early Christian times only the wealthy could afford the pilgrimage to Rome and common Englishmen had to rest content with visiting a local shrine. Even then the choice of shrines must have been wide, with the memory of the foundation of their churches still fresh in the minds of the people, and the relics of hundreds of founders ('saints') close at hand, especially in Wales and Cornwall. By the time pilgrimage reached its heyday in the 14th century the phenomenon was enormous. The recorded numbers of pilgrims to Canterbury for many years exceeded 200,000, out of a total population in England estimated at just under four million on the outbreak of the Black Death in 1348.

The number of famous shrines grew and grew as monks and prelates vied to attract more pilgrims. Every single church was supposed to have a relic of some kind. Many judged the fame of towns, not on the size of the population or the quality of their products, but on the number and reputation of their relics. Some shrines had connections with numerous saints: 13 at Glastonbury. Other monasteries and churches possessed more relics than they knew what to do with – over 400 were said to exist at Canterbury, where 250 miracles were described in the six years after St Thomas's death.

The pilgrim, who had a home to return to, was distinct from the palmer, who had none. He was a professional pilgrim, living on nothing but alms and perpetually journeying from

ABOVE: Pilgrims contemporary with Geoffrey Chaucer make their way to the Holy Land in this illumination from a 14th-century manuscript on the Crusades.

shrine to shrine. Men knew him by the palm or branch brought back from the Holy Land itself. Of course being a palmer was a most convenient cover for all kinds of escaped villeins and criminals, or those who found a settled existence or their fellow men too much to bear. In a word, some of them were tramps, adept at putting the evil eye on those common souls who shunned them.

If a man was too sick, or busy, or lazy to go on pilgrimage for himself, it was common to employ a proxy to do the journey on his behalf, and the Church prudently recognised this as just as effective as making the journey himself. More commonly the proxy pilgrimage took place after death to gain some favour on the Day of Judgement; funds would be specified by will for the purpose.

People had many different motives for going on a pilgrimage. Mostly they went for religious reasons, but often the dominant factor was more secular. The most common motive was to pray at the shrine, appealing directly to the saint for success in a venture, which might be business, love, war or an attempt to throw off an illness or

ABOVE: *The King's headstrong knights murder Archbishop Becket as he prays at a side altar in Canterbury Cathedral on 29 December 1170, depicted in an almost contemporary psalter.*

disability. Vows made at home, in a church or even in the heat of battle often obliged the believer to make long journeys as a thanksgiving for safe deliverance.

The obligatory gifts to the shrine gave the Church a truly vast income, and such was the prestige and wealth conferred on a church by the major miracle-working relics that theft of relics and outright fraud by monks were widespread in the Middle Ages.

ABOVE: *A 12th-century stained-glass window of St Thomas Becket in Canterbury Cathedral, made a few years after the archbishop's martyrdom.*

LEFT & RIGHT: *A group of monks (left) and crusaders on horseback, from the 14th-century Chronicle of St Denis.*

✠ The Celtic Saints

The Celtic Church was a bastion of learning and artistic endeavour in a barbarous Europe and its contacts were international. The early monks moved at will around the seaways of western Britain – Dumnonia (the Cornish peninsula), Wales and Dalriada (the west of Scotland) – Ireland and Brittany, exploiting their common language. In those times any learned man who successfully founded a new church was likely to be canonised after a decent interval by his congregation – St Carantoc in Cornwall is an example. Such was the independence of each community under the Celtic rule. Energetic monks like Patrick, Columba, David or Piran were held in such esteem by their brethren and spiritual children that their churches soon became shrines to their memory and pilgrims braved every hardship to gain wisdom, guidance, comfort or healing from their physical remains. Among these inspiring figures, some are remembered for their extraordinary spirituality and some for the strangeness of their legends.

Columba is famous as the monk who evangelised Scotland, but this happened almost by accident. He was an Irish prince, born about 521,

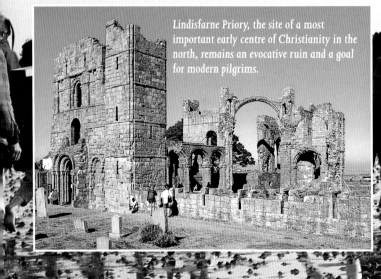

LEFT: *St John, seen in the Lindisfarne Gospels (c. AD 698), the most precious wo of art to survive from early Christian Englan*

who became a follower of St Patrick. His character might be considered unsaintly: his actions show that he was forceful, stubborn and ambitious. In about 563 Columba's refusal to give up a manuscript, the Vulgate Gospels, culminated in vast bloodshed at the Battle of Cul Dremne. Regretting his stubbornness, he vowed to leave Ireland and never return. Columba sailed to Iona and was soon taking the word across the sea to the pagans of Mull and beyond into Argyll. There he converted the ruling house of Dalriada and then carried his mission all over Scotland. Following his death on Iona in 597, pilgrims came to venerate his relics in the church there.

Cuthbert was a shepherd boy from the Lammermuir Hills in the Scottish Lowlands. In 651, at the age of about 16, he entered the Celtic monastery of Melrose. Later in life he was prior of Lindisfarne (Holy Island) but wherever he served he was to go on long missionary journeys, preaching in remote villages and farmsteads in the hills. Returning to Lindisfarne, he would retire to the solitude of a hermitage on the bare slab of rock in the sea near the priory which still bears the name

Lindisfarne Priory, the site of a most important early centre of Christianity in the north, remains an evocative ruin and a goal for modern pilgrims.

St Cuthbert's Isle. In 676, as a result of his 'long and spotless active life', he was allowed by his abbot and monks the special privilege of retiring to 'the stillness of divine contemplation' on one of the Farne Islands off the Northumbrian coast. In about 698, eleven years after his death and burial at Lindisfarne, the monks elevated his body to a new shrine and discovered its incorruption: the body had not decayed and the saint appeared as if asleep. From that time onward, it was an object of

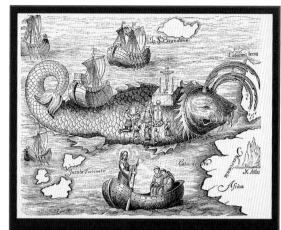

Brendan's Voyage and Patrick

There are many legends about St Patrick and his conversion of Ireland in the 5th century (see pages 26–7). As a youth, he was enslaved by raiders in Ireland but he escaped, and spent many years in France. Patrick, impelled by recurrent dreams, was over 60 when he began his mission to Ireland. Later, an Irish monk called Brendan (c.486–575) made a voyage by coracle (a light boat covered in skins), perhaps even reaching North America. The Voyage of St Brendan enjoyed great popularity in the Middle Ages. It is a curious allegory of discovery combined with mysticism, sometimes describing nature in minute detail.

ABOVE: *An early Christian monastery was founded at Glendalough in County Wicklow by St Kevin, who died in 618. The remains include a round tower used for refuge in times of danger.*

BELOW: *The 8th-century St John's Cross stands outside Iona's restored church, on the site of the monastery used by St Columba as a base for converting Scotland to Christianity.*

special veneration. Cuthbert's cult was already well established by the end of the 7th century and he has remained Northumbria's favourite saint ever since. The body, its shrine and the famous Lindisfarne Gospels began a long journey to a new home when the Vikings threatened Lindisfarne in 875. Only in 995 did they find a permanent home at Durham, where a Saxon church was specially built for them and consecrated three years later.

Pilgrims walking across the mudflats to the tidal island of Lindisfarne (Holy Island), once the retreat of St Cuthbert and his monks.

✠ The Celtic Saints

David, or **Dewi Sant** in Welsh, is the patron saint of Wales who gave his name to the peninsula, Dewisland, containing his shrine, cathedral and city. The historical David is difficult to pin down because we are unsure how much written about his life by later chroniclers is distortion or sheer invention. As with the life of St Patrick, there is an almost complete lack of contemporary witness. We know for certain that David was a native Welshman who lived in the 6th century, and a great missionary and founder of monasteries in his country. He is said to have come from a royal line. According to legend, his mother was St Non, a nun at Ty Gwyn near Whitesands Bay, Pembrokeshire, who was seduced by Prince Sant and then spent the rest of her life in prayer and self-mortification. However, it is possible that she became a nun in widowhood after David's birth.

At David's baptism a fountain of the purest water burst forth spontaneously for the rite (this is now St Non's Well, a mile from St Davids Cathedral), while a blind monk holding the infant received his sight. After founding monasteries all over the land, David chose Vallis Rosina for his main community, which grew into the influential

RIGHT: St David's shrine, in his cathedral at the remote end of Pembrokeshire, is graced by his restored reliquary, found walled up during 19th-century restoration work.

BELOW: The peace and simplicity of St Non's Chapel, restored in the local early Christian style, evokes the spirit of St David, born at this place on the Pembrokeshire coast in the 6th century.

monastery and diocese of St Davids. David died and was buried in his own monastery. It is believed that his relics still exist in an ancient oak and iron casket which is now displayed in a stone niche behind the high altar – the very place, in fact, where the clergy hid them in the 16th century. A beautiful wrought-iron screen thwarts latter-day relic thieves. To see this shrine resplendent with daffodils, pilgrims should visit the cathedral on St David's Day (1 March).

In the 7th century, according to the myth, a young Welsh prince called Caradoc tried to seduce the virgin **Winefrede**. Failing in his objective but still inflamed with lust, he cut off her head 'which falling to the earth, deserved of God to have a fountain of water to spring in the place, which to this day continueth'. Her tutor, Beuno, came out of

> Who would true valour see,
> Let him come hither;
> One here will constant be,
> Come wind, come weather.
> There's no discouragement
> Shall make him once relent
> His first avowed intent
> To be a pilgrim.
>
> THE PILGRIM'S PROGRESS, JOHN BUNYAN

St Michael's Mount, a mystical island off the coast of Cornwall, was the scene of two visions of the Archangel Michael and site of a Benedictine monastery.

the nearby church and discovering the calamity, cursed Caradoc so that the ground swallowed him up. Then taking Winefrede's head into Mass and calling on his people for their prayers, Beuno joined the head back with the body. Not only did Winefrede miraculously survive but she lived on for another 15 years.

This legend was only written down by an unknown monk in the 12th century. Six centuries later, in the Age of Reason, Dr William Fleetwood, Bishop of St Asaph, loathed this pilgrimage in his diocese and condemned it, declaring that he could not believe a story recorded 500 years after the subject's death. On the other hand, Winefrede seems very much like a pagan legend in a Christian dress. The story of a severed head miraculously rejoined to a body which springs back to life is typical of the often dark Celtic imagination and occurs several times in Celtic mythology.

ABOVE: The annual pilgrimage to St Winefrede's Well, the site of the saint's martyrdom at Holywell in Flintshire, north Wales. Winefrede's is the only pilgrimage to have survived unchecked through the Reformation. Her sacred well is the most complete medieval shrine in Britain.

9

✠ The Pilgrim Routes
Canterbury † Rome † Jerusalem † Santiago

The greatest pilgrimage in medieval times was to Jerusalem. After the Muslim conquest of Palestine in the 7th century, genuine pilgrims continued to travel to the Holy Sepulchre, the traditional site of Christ's burial. But the journey was difficult and dangerous, not to say expensive. During the Crusades, the few pilgrims who ventured on the journey needed the Knights Hospitaller to succour them and the Knights Templar to defend them.

Crowds throng the Plaza de Obradoiro, dominated by the riotous 18th-century façade of the famous shrine of St James the Greater at Santiago de Compostela. Since medieval times the faithful have worn the cockleshell (inset) to symbolise their successful completion of this pilgrimage.

ABOVE: The south door of the Holy Sepulchre in Jerusalem, the traditional site of Christ's crucifixion, burial and resurrection. This shrine, the most rewarding of all possible Christian pilgrimages, is now shared between the many denominations.

Many pilgrims preferred a safer and cheaper option. For those willing to travel beyond their own country the most popular destinations were to the seven pilgrimage churches of Rome and the shrine of the apostle, St James the Greater, at Santiago de Compostela in Galicia (north-west Spain). Sometimes the Pope decreed, in a Papal Bull, the relative value of shrines to the pilgrim's soul; for example, Pope Calixtus II granted that two pilgrimages to St Davids in Pembrokeshire were equal to one pilgrimage to Rome; or in Latin, *Roma semel quantum, Dat bis Menevia tantum.*

The Pilgrims' Way

The most popular pilgrimage during the Middle Ages was along the Pilgrims' Way from Winchester to Canterbury, to the shrine of England's most famous saint and martyr, St Thomas Becket. The archbishop's brutal and shocking murder, after his quarrel with King Henry II, led to his canonisation on Ash Wednesday in 1173. The largest number of medieval miracles in Britain occurred in the name of St Thomas.

Geoffrey Chaucer's *Canterbury Tales*, composed in about 1390, describes with wry humour the journey of a group of worldly pilgrims from London to Canterbury. Chaucer reveals a lack of esteem for the monastic life and the cult of relics, an increasingly common attitude in his day.

Less well-known than Picaud's work is the itinerary of Sigeric, an Anglo-Saxon Archbishop of Canterbury who went on a pilgrimage to Rome in 990 to collect his pallium (mantle of office) from Pope John XV. A clerk or cleric in his retinue recorded all 80 stages of their journey. So it is possible to trace the exact route the 10th-century pilgrim followed from England to Rome. Following Sigeric's route today leads to the discovery of numerous relics of the roads and their medieval traffic in the form of wayside crosses, especially elaborate wayside shrines, old street names and accommodation built for the faithful by religious orders or town guilds.

The main roads to major medieval shrines achieved quite a high degree of organisation, with pilgrims forming convoys to travel from one hospice or inn to another.

The best-known account of life on the road and a specific pilgrimage is the *Codex Calixtenus*, edited by Aymery Picaud in about 1150. In five books he describes three routes from France which all combine at the Pyrenees to conduct the faithful to the shrine of St James of Compostela. This hallowed route across northern Spain to Santiago offers the modern traveller, whether as a pilgrim or as an historian, the most satisfying experience of any of the old pilgrimages.

ABOVE: *A medieval map of Christendom showing Jerusalem at the centre of the world. Pilgrims to the Holy Land faced many dangers and were protected on the journey by the knights of the Crusades.*

LEFT: *Medieval pilgrims in front of the Holy Sepulchre in Jerusalem, from the Book of Marvels, on the travels of Marco Polo. They wear traditional costume and one of them makes a donation to the shrine.*

✠ The Pilgrim's Journey

The first stage in the medieval pilgrim's journey was usually the ceremony of leaving his home parish. After Mass and special prayers, the priest consecrated the pilgrim's scrip (a wallet similar to a modern fishing bag) and bourdon (his tall staff), sprinkling each with holy water. Then his friends and relatives led him out of the village with the cross borne high before them and gave him their blessing at the parish boundary. He would also carry a letter from his priest or his temporal lord to act as a recommendation of his genuine status to the pious and charitable.

How would he be recognised on the road? To wear the pilgrim's costume was both an honour and a penance, which served to identify him and help in begging for alms along the way. He wore a long and coarse woollen robe, brown or russet in colour and big enough to wrap around him for sleeping. A cross decorated the sleeve. His large round hat had a broad brim, usually turned up at the front to display his pilgrim badges – the symbolic shell and leaden images from the shrines he had already visited. Slung on lanyards around his neck he carried a scrip, a large knife, a flask for water and a rosary. The scrip was for spare pairs of hosen (stockings), two day's food and essential ointment for the feet. Finally, he carried a long stout staff, used for vaulting over streams, climbing hills and as defence against outlaws. It might be tipped with a hollow metal ball, the jangling 'Canterbury bell'.

Pilgrimage was largely a summer occupation and presumably people often slept under hedges or in barns. The accommodation which survives in England from the heyday of pilgrimage varies from hospices run by monks or a dedicated charity, to monasteries whose rules obliged the brethren to offer hospitality to any traveller, and common inns. The Hospital of Newark at Maidstone was a fine example of a hospice supported by a charity. Archbishop Boniface built it in 1261 to receive pilgrims to

ABOVE: *White Hart Cottage at Compton, in Surrey, is by tradition a former pilgrims' hospice* INSET: *Geoffrey Chaucer.*

Pilgrim Crosses

Wayside crosses served as waymarks to reassure travellers that they were on the right road and as roadside shrines, where they could offer prayers for a safe journey. Old maps and records indicate where some of them once stood. They were often sited where they could be seen from a great distance, at old crossroads on a pilgrim route. Most of these have disappeared but two fine examples survive on the route to the shrine of Our Lady at Walsingham: Binham Cross on the road from the miraculous Holy Rood of Bromholme, and Hockley cum Wilton Cross on the road from Ely.

LEFT: *A Canterbury pilgrim leaves the city past the great Benedictine Abbey of St Augustine, from the 15th-century Poetry of John Lydgate.*

BELOW RIGHT: *A leaden pilgrim badge in the form of the head of St Thomas Becket, of the type sold to visitors as tokens of their pilgrimage to Canterbury. The badge (in the Royal Museum & Art Gallery, Canterbury) was a vital part of the medieval pilgrim's costume.*

The Pilgrim's Progress

John Bunyan rose from humble origins as a tinker to become one of the world's best-known and popular Christian writers. His *Pilgrim's Progress*, first published in 1678, is now read in more than 200 languages. Bunyan found that he had a gift for preaching, as well as free-thinking. His activities, however, landed him in Bedford County Gaol for 12 years. There he 'dreamed a dream' and wrote his famous book about a pilgrimage through the Slough of Despond, Vanity Fair, the Hill of Difficulty and onwards to the Celestial City.

BELOW: *A pilgrim travels with the customary scrip (pouch) and staff, in an illustration from John Bunyan's famous tale.*

Canterbury, although it is several miles from the Pilgrims' Way. Now only its Early English chapel survives and is in use as the chancel of St Peter's church.

Canterbury had many hospices, such as the Hospital of St Thomas the Martyr, now known as the King's Bridge Hospital and founded, according to its charter, by the 'glorious St Thomas the Martyr to receive poor wayfaring men'. The Norman crypt and later refectory and chapel can still be seen. Other pilgrims lodged in the great priory of Christ Church (the cathedral), where a 15th-century extension known as Chillenden Guest Chamber survives as part of the Bishop of Dover's house. Smaller numbers dispersed to the Hospital of St John in Northgate, the great Augustinian abbey or guest houses run by the mendicant friars.

The motley group of worldly pilgrims in Geoffrey Chaucer's Canterbury Tales, shown on the road in a modern frieze (Royal Museum & Art Gallery, Canterbury).

☩ Walking the Pilgrim Ways

Stand at the crossroads and look,
Ask for the ancient paths,
Ask where the good way is,
And walk in it,
And you will find rest for your souls.

HOLY BIBLE, JEREMIAH 6:16

The wide expanses of the
Wiltshire Downs, close to the
prehistoric Harrow Way, an
ancient route across southern
Britain.

Modern pilgrims often travel by car or coach to a popular shrine such as St Thomas at Canterbury or Our Lady at Walsingham, yet there are many who still prefer to go on foot. They are to be seen, especially, on the Way of St James in the north of Spain. In Britain, our inspiration comes from the writer Hilaire Belloc, who wore the three mantles of faithful pilgrim, observant local historian and incorrigible trespasser. He trudged from Alsace to the Vatican and left us a witty account in *The Path to Rome* (1902). Then he muddied his boots on our own Pilgrims' Way from Winchester to Canterbury, describing what remained to be seen from medieval times and merrily theorising as only he could in *The Old Road* (1904). Since then there have been several other guidebooks to The Pilgrims' Way and plenty of authors have written about miracles, relics and the architecture of pilgrimage.

For full descriptions of the suggested walks along the traditional pilgrim ways, see Keith Sugden's book *Walking the Pilgrim Ways* (1989, David & Charles).

Pilgrim Routes

Old Sarum to Glastonbury
Cirencester to Bath
Oban to Iona
Hexham to Lindisfarne
St Piran's Cell to St Michael's Mount
Llanfihangel Abercowin to St Davids
  Cathedral
Winchester to Canterbury
Beverley Minster to York Minster
St Asaph to St Winefrede's, Holywell
Ely to Walsingham

TOP: *Walkers who follow the old pilgrim routes will discover the many joys of the British countryside, such as this ancient Cotswold bridge, which marks the spot where the Roman Fosse Way crosses the infant River Avon.*

LEFT: *Chaucer's much-married Wife of Bath, who told a bawdy story during her ride to the shrine of St Thomas. An illumination from the Ellesmere Manuscript.*

✚ Saints & Shrines

Beverley † Canterbury † Chester

Medieval beliefs about relics are central to pilgrimage. Relics inspired the medieval faithful with a sense of power and mystery. The power suffused the physical remains that a holy person left behind on earth, and the supplicants could, by adoring the relics, gain the intercession of the saint in their lives. So the saints were simultaneously present in heaven and in their earthly relics. If a saint's relics were divided and dispersed to other churches, their power was not diminished; a finger bone was as precious as a whole body.

A relic was kept for its own security, and for its greater glory, in a shrine, a term which refers specifically to its receptacle (*scrinium*). More generally, the term means the shrine-base with its elaborate superstructure and cover which surround the small jewelled reliquary. More widely, shrine refers to a holy place, such as Canterbury Cathedral.

ABOVE: *A 13th-century stained-glass window in the Trinity Chapel at Canterbury Cathedral shows pilgrims worshipping at the splendid shrine to St Thomas Becket.*

England has some big parish churches but none is quite as huge as **Beverley Minster**. And at Beverley it is not just the size which impresses, for here there is a standard of design, masonry and sculpture far higher than at many of England's medieval cathedrals.

John of Beverley had the honour of ordaining the Venerable Bede, famous chronicler of early Christian times. Later he became Bishop of York. Among his many cures was that of a deaf and dumb boy: so famous is this miracle that he is remembered today as the patron saint of the deaf and dumb. Following his death in 721 St John's relics rested in a magnificent shrine in the ambulatory behind the high altar at Beverley, the most usual place in a large medieval church. Pilgrims would have approached along the choir aisles. The relics were moved to the nave after the shrine's destruction at the Reformation.

Pilgrims to the medieval shrine of **St Thomas Becket** in **Canterbury Cathedral** found themselves

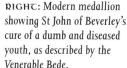

The twin west towers and the great central tower ('Bell Harry') still rise above the city of Canterbury to welcome pilgrims to Britain's most famous shrine.

RIGHT: Modern medallion showing St John of Beverley's cure of a dumb and diseased youth, as described by the Venerable Bede.

RIGHT: A 14th-century bench-end in Chester Cathedral's splendid choir shows a pilgrim with his staff and characteristic hat.

well organised. Monks met them, marshalled them into orderly groups and conducted them into the cathedral through the very same door in the north transept used by both Becket and his attackers on 29 December 1170. The first station was the spot where Thomas was brutally cut down, the whole scene no doubt vividly described by the practised guide, as the pilgrims knelt on the cold flags and looked in horror on the tip of de Brito's sword, shattered by the mighty blow that had split the martyr's skull in two.

The second station was the high altar where the body lay throughout the fatal night. Finally the pilgrims descended to the Norman crypt and prayed at the miraculous tomb itself. On 7 July 1220 the relics were translated (moved) to their new shrine behind the high altar in the new Gothic cathedral. As it was the most famous shrine in the kingdom, Henry VIII's commissioners took special care to destroy everything at the Reformation.

St Werburgh, whose shrine is found in the Lady Chapel in **Chester Cathedral**, was the daughter of Wulfere, the Saxon king of Mercia. She became a nun and, through her piety, an abbess noted for her reforms. After she died, in the early 8th century at her nunnery of Trentham, many miracles were reported from her tomb at Hanbury in Staffordshire. Her relics came to Chester to protect them from ravages by the Danes. The church was then a minster, specially enlarged to house her relics. After the Norman Conquest it was rebuilt again, following its conversion to a Benedictine abbey. Werburgh's shrine remained a great centre of pilgrimage until the Reformation; part of its stone base survives in today's cathedral. Her main emblem in art is a goose, which, according to Goscelin's *Life*, she was supposed to have restored to life.

17

✠ Saints & Shrines

Chichester † Durham † Ely

Marc Chagall's 1978 stained-glass window in the north of the retrochoir, illustrating Psalm 150, greets modern pilgrims to Chichester Cathedral, site of the shrine of St Richard until the Reformation.

Richard of Wych, bishop of **Chichester** 1245–53, was born at Droitwich in 1197, the son of a yeoman farmer. He studied in the universities of Oxford, Paris and Bologna. In 1235 he returned to Oxford to lecture in canon law and soon became chancellor. Following his ordination in 1242, he became priest in the Kent parishes of Charing and Deal. In 1244 he was elected bishop of Chichester, but Henry III and part of the chapter refused to accept him. After an appeal to the authority of Rome, Pope Innocent IV consecrated Richard bishop at Lyons. Besides being a model diocesan bishop, Richard enthusiastically preached the crusades, not as a political expedition, but as a means of making access to the Holy Land easier for pilgrims. He was canonised in 1262 and his relics were translated to a splendid new shrine behind the high altar in his cathedral in 1276. The shrine was despoiled by Henry VIII's commissioners in 1538, when Richard's body was reburied secretly. In art, he is depicted with a chalice at his feet, in memory of the occasion when he dropped the chalice at Mass, but the wine miraculously remained unspilt.

The cult and fame of **St Cuthbert** was responsible for the rebuilding of **Durham Cathedral** in the magnificent Norman style. In about 1140 an attempt by Bishop de Puiset to build a Lady Chapel at the east end failed due to subsidence but this was attributed to the displeasure of St Cuthbert, buried nearby. As a result, the bishop built at the west end the Romanesque Galilee Chapel. In these surroundings, unique in England, the cult of St Cuthbert flourished. A huge catalogue of wealth accumulated but it was all surrendered to the crown in 1540, along with the monastery. Following the destruction of his shrine, St Cuthbert was reburied on the same spot beneath a plain marble slab.

The Venerable Bede describes the life of the saint who founded **Ely Cathedral**. Despite two noble marriages, **Etheldreda** remained a virgin and retreated to an island in the Fens which had been part of the dowry of her first marriage. There she founded a nunnery in 673 and died in 679. Sixteen years after Etheldreda's burial, her body was found free from decay – then seen as the surest sign of sanctity. In the 13th century the east end of the great cathedral was rebuilt to honour her tomb – before the Reformation her shrine was in the place of honour immediately in front of the high altar.

BELOW: *The tomb of St Cuthbert, the north of England's most popular saint, behind the high altar of Durham Cathedral, where he was reburied during the Reformation.*

LEFT INSET: *Cuthbert's precious garnet-and-gold Pectoral Cross, dating from the 7th century.*

Fragments from the base of the shrine can still be seen next to the tomb of Bishop Hugh de Northwold who extended the cathedral. The translation of her body to its new shrine is observed on 17 October, St Etheldreda's Fair, vulgarly called St Awdry's Fair. So cheap and showy was the finery, especially lace, sold there that the contraction of 'St Awdry' gives us the English word 'tawdry'. But there is nothing tawdry about the marvellous cathedral, with its famous 'Octagon' tower, which rises like a huge ship above the Fens and the little buildings of this well-preserved old market town.

ABOVE: *The choir at Ely Cathedral, rebuilt in honour of the founder, St Etheldreda, in the 13th century. Her shrine stood, rather unusually, in front of the high altar between the choir stalls.*

☩ Saints & Shrines
Hereford † Lichfield † Lincoln

Thomas Cantelupe, known as St Thomas of Hereford, was born in 1218 at Hambledon in Buckinghamshire into a noble and powerful Norman family. His uncle, the bishop of Worcester, supervised his education and prepared Thomas for high office in both church and state. He went to study in Oxford, Paris and Orleans, returning, like St Richard of Chichester before him, to be chancellor at Oxford. Following the defeat of Henry III at the Battle of Lewes, Thomas became chancellor of England for a year until Simon de Montfort's defeat at the Battle of Evesham. He left the country and returned to Paris as lecturer in canon law. In 1275 the canons of Hereford elected him their bishop but Thomas soon quarrelled violently with John Pecham, Archbishop of Canterbury. He found himself excommunicated and resorted to the papal court at Orvieto in central Italy, but died on 25 August 1282 at Montefiascone. He was buried at Orvieto but his heart and bones were returned to Hereford Cathedral. How the shrine survived the Reformation is a mystery.

Chad, a much-loved monk, was brought out of retirement in his monastery to be Bishop of Mercia in 669. The Venerable Bede recounts, in his History of the English Church and People, written in 731, that Chad died of disease on 2 March 672,

an event foretold by a choir of angels seven days earlier at **Lichfield**, where his cult has since remained. Bede says that he was first buried in St Mary's Church, then in St Peter's. At both shrines frequent miracles of healing attested to Chad's virtues. In 1148 the relics were translated to a shrine at the high altar of the Norman cathedral. The cult was so popular that in 1330, at a cost of £2000, Bishop Langton built another shrine, placed behind the high altar for easier access to pilgrims. The site is still marked today.

ABOVE: St Chad preferred to make his missionary journeys around Mercia on foot. In this Victorian roundel at Lichfield Cathedral, Archbishop Theodore instructs him to ride a horse around his diocese.

LEFT: Few medieval shrines escaped destruction by Henry VIII's commissioners, though St Thomas Cantelupe's survived, in the north transept of Hereford Cathedral. Set on a pedestal of Purbeck marble, the niches at the base of the shrine contain statues of fourteen Knights Templar. The saint was their provincial grand master.

Lincoln Cathedral's glorious Angel Choir, built for the growing number of pilgrims attracted to St Hugh's shrine, takes its name from the 30 carved angels in the triforium spandrels. Queen Eleanor attended its consecration in 1280.

Such a fine cathedral also acquired other relics: the Sacrist's Roll for 1345 lists 'the relics of divers saints...some of the bones of St Laurence, some of Golgotha...part of the sepulchre of the Blessed Virgin Mary...part of the finger and cowl of St William, some of the bones of St Stephen...'. Episodes in Chad's life are shown in six panels of stained glass in the Chapter House and in a Victorian tiled floor by Minton in the presbytery.

Hugh was a strong-minded and zealous bishop at **Lincoln** who survived an argument with Henry I over the excommunication of a royal forester. Hugh was conspicuous by his unbounded charity, especially towards lepers, and his efforts in rebuilding the cathedral. His funeral was held during a council of state at Lincoln in 1200: among the bearers were King John of England and King William of Scotland. In 1280 Hugh's body was translated in splendour to a golden shrine in the place of honour in the glorious Angel Choir. The head graced a separate golden *chef* (reliquary in the shape of a head) nearby. The scale of the pilgrimage to his shrine was then second only to St Thomas at Canterbury. Lincoln also boasted three other shrines, those of Little St Hugh and two more bishops, Robert Grosseteste and John of Dalderby.

21

✠ Saints & Shrines
Ripon † St Alban's † St Edmundsbury † Salisbury

A new Anglican diocese was created in 1836 at an attractive market town in rural Yorkshire. Only then did **Ripon** Minster become a cathedral. Today it is a mixture of styles. It has a Saxon crypt and displays in its parts the development of the Romanesque and Gothic styles. The cathedral contains the shrine of **St Wilfrid**. He was the robust protagonist whose arguments defeated the Celtic partisans, or followers of St Columba, at the Synod of Whitby in 664. Elected Bishop of York, he converted the Northumbrian church to the Roman custom and introduced the Benedictine rule to northern monasteries. After an argument over the division of his see, he fell from power, appealed to the Pope (the first time an English bishop did this) and was finally restored to

BELOW: A detail of the modern window in the Pilgrim Chapel at Ripon Cathedral commemorates the cult of St Wilfrid, which flourished in the former minster. The crypt of Wilfrid's church is a rare survival.

RIGHT: The shrine of St Alban, destroyed in the Reformation and now reconstructed from 2,000 fragments. Behind it is the rare oak watching loft, used by monks who guarded the shrine and relics.

his monastery at Ripon, where he was buried in 709.

St Alban is honoured as Britain's first martyr (c.209), suffering his fate for sheltering a Christian priest fleeing the persecution of Septimus Severus. According to legend the executioner's eyes fell out as his sword struck off the head. Passionate debates arose about St Alban's bones. In the two centuries between the Norman Conquest and the account by the monk Matthew Paris so many lies had been told about the saint's relics that it became difficult for anyone to claim that they had the bones of the protomartyr if, indeed, they had ever been preserved. The elaborate and richly bejewelled shrine of c.1302–08 was destroyed in 1539 but two thousand fragments of its tall pedestal of Purbeck marble were discovered in 1872, built into a wall blocking off the east end of the church. Painstakingly reassembled then, and again in 1991, it still gives a hint of the richness of this most worldly of medieval abbeys, although its canopy was destroyed at the Reformation.

Edmund, a Saxon prince, inherited the throne of the East Angles at the age of 15, at a time when the incursions of the Danes were increasing. According to tradition, the young Edmund fought the Danes in 869 at the battle of Thetford. Dismayed by the carnage of his people, he surrendered himself to the enemy in the hope that the sacrifice of his own life might save his subjects. After a severe beating, he was tied naked to a tree, scourged with whips, riddled with arrows and finally beheaded. A legend says that the discarded head was found by a wolf, who followed the funeral procession at Hoxne until the head was rejoined to the body. Thirty-three years later, following a series of miracles, the relics were translated to a shrine at Bury, where the cult of the last king of East Anglia flourished. Although the arms

ABOVE: *This detail from a hanging embroidered by Sybil Andrews in 1975 shows Edmund, king and martyr, shot by Danish bowmen during their invasion. Also depicted is the legendary wolf who guarded Edmund's head.*

BELOW: *This tomb is traditionally identified as part of the medieval shrine of St Osmund, whose body was moved from Old Sarum and reinterred at the new Salisbury Cathedral in 1226.*

of the city of Bury St Edmunds incorporate a wolf's head to this day, the site of the shrine is now lost and very little remains of the once gigantic abbey.

According to a 15th-century document, **Osmund**, bishop of Old Sarum 1078–99, was a nephew of William the Conqueror and came to England as chaplain with the Duke's army in 1066. This may well be true, as he was employed by the king in a civil capacity to prepare part of the Domesday Book. He was also present at the consecration of Battle Abbey. He perhaps even held the chancellorship before being consecrated bishop of Old Sarum in 1078. He himself consecrated the new **Salisbury** cathedral on the hilltop in 1092 and was active in establishing a Norman chapter and hierarchy. Later, his *Use of Sarum*, a service book, met with almost universal acceptance in Britain and Ireland. Osmund was canonised in 1457.

✤ Saints & Shrines

Westminster † Winchester † Worcester † York

Westminster Abbey still venerates the shrine of King **Edward the Confessor**, builder of the late Saxon abbey. The well-documented reconstruction by Henry III further elevated the status of this royal shrine. In 1241 he ordered a new monument to be made of gold and marble. Both king and queen presented jewels or money for the extremely lavish work. This great shrine survives, stripped of valuables but surrounded by the tombs of most of England's medieval kings. Nearby in the abbey, the tomb of Henry VII was almost an official shrine. The tomb of this king, a usurper who defeated Richard III at the Battle of Bosworth, serves the purpose of legitimising his Tudor regime.

RIGHT: *The shrine of Edward the Confessor in Westminster Abbey was briefly dismantled during the Reformation. It probably escaped destruction because Henry VIII claimed kinship with Edward. The tombs of England's medieval kings and queens surround the shrine.*

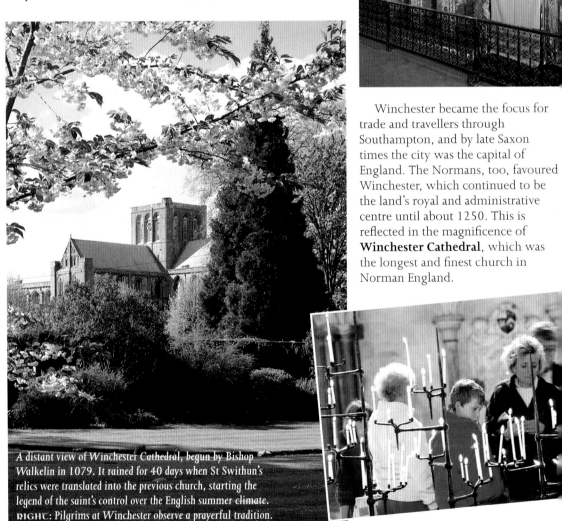

Winchester became the focus for trade and travellers through Southampton, and by late Saxon times the city was the capital of England. The Normans, too, favoured Winchester, which continued to be the land's royal and administrative centre until about 1250. This is reflected in the magnificence of **Winchester Cathedral**, which was the longest and finest church in Norman England.

A distant view of Winchester Cathedral, begun by Bishop Walkelin in 1079. It rained for 40 days when St Swithun's relics were translated into the previous church, starting the legend of the saint's control over the English summer climate.
RIGHT: *Pilgrims at Winchester observe a prayerful tradition.*

Quite apart from its strategic and political importance, the 12th-century city had famous 'workshops' of carving and manuscript illumination. The Winchester School was one of the great triumphs of English artistic genius. It was also esteemed for the shrine of **St Swithun**, its 9th-century bishop during the period of the great monastic reforms under St Dunstan. This pilgrimage site was highly popular long before the murder of Thomas Becket in 1170. Only a few fragments remain of the medieval shrine but the cathedral continues to be the starting point for the Pilgrims' Way to Canterbury.

As an esteemed novice, **Wulfstan** was admitted as a monk to **Worcester** cathedral-monastery before the Norman Conquest. Rising to be prior under the bishop, he travelled about baptising the children of the poor because, it is said, the secular clergy refused to do this without a fee. Wulfstan made himself useful to King Harold but then swiftly made submission to William the Conqueror at Berkhampstead. In 1088, he denounced English and Welsh rebels marching on Worcester, thereby, according to tradition, securing their defeat. He was buried at Worcester and immediately regarded as a saint, although he was not formally canonised until 1203. King John on his deathbed commended his soul to God and St Wulfstan and was buried next to the shrine.

William Fitzherbert was of noble birth, the son of Herbert, Henry I's treasurer, and had a luxurious upbringing, probably at the Norman royal court in Winchester. When the Archbishop of York, Thurstan, died in 1140, a furious and prolonged dispute arose about the succession, involving King Stephen, the Cistercians at Fountains

LEFT: *Wulfstan offering his church. Parts of Wulfstan's cathedral at Worcester, built in the Romanesque style, still survive, and include the largest Norman crypt in England.*

Abbey, the Archbishop of Canterbury, the great St Bernard of Clairvaux and Pope Innocent II. When William finally became archbishop, tragedy struck within a month. He was seized with a sudden illness while celebrating Mass in his own minster. Poisoning was suspected and antidotes were administered at once but to no avail. William died eight days later, with Archdeacon Osbert accused of poisoning the eucharistic chalice. William was admitted to the calendar of saints in 1227.

RIGHT: *St William of York, a minor figure promoted in life beyond his abilities and in death beyond his miracles, from the Bolton Hours, c.1420, in York Minster Library.*

✠ Survival and Revival

Holywell in North Wales is a shrine where the adherents of the old faith never let go. During the Middle Ages this ancient pagan well became one of the most popular Christian places of pilgrimage due to the legend of St Winefrede. During the Reformation, for reasons which remain obscure, it also became a focus of activity by Catholic recusants (nonconformists). Pilgrims never stopped coming to the shrine, despite the best efforts of the Anglican bishop and the civil authorities. Today the shrine is still visited by thousands of pilgrims every year; not too many to destroy the peace of this most ornamental of Gothic chapels, but enough to keep the candles burning constantly.

At Walsingham, during the 20th century, both Anglicans and Catholics have revived the pilgrimage of medieval kings, each maintaining a separate shrine, but neither on the original sacred site. Canterbury, too, has benefited from this modern enthusiasm for an old custom. More genuine pilgrims now arrive at the shrine of St Thomas Becket than at any time since 1500.

In the far west of Ireland, there are three shrines with an even stronger hold on their devotees. Nowhere else in the British Isles is pilgrimage

ABOVE: *The annual procession to the Anglican shrine of Our Lady of Walsingham in Norfolk, a medieval pilgrimage vigorously revived in the 20th century by Catholic, Protestant and Orthodox Christians.*

taken more seriously than at Lough Derg in county Donegal, where pilgrims assemble on St Patrick's Island on the saint's day for an extremely rigorous three-day penance to commemorate his fast. Croagh Patrick is a mountain of rock and scree on the Atlantic coast of county Mayo, where St Patrick meditated for 40 days and prayed that Ireland should remain forever Christian. On the last

St Patrick's Island in Lough Derg, County Donegal, is the scene of the most rigorous pilgrimage in Britain or Ireland, where devotees assemble for a strict three-day penance on the saint's day.

A picturesque French town nestling at the foot of the Pyrenees receives five million visitors a year. They come here because of the most famous vision of modern times. On 11 February 1858, a poor girl aged 14 years, Bernadette Soubirous, met and later spoke with the Virgin Mary in a cave called Massabielle. The vision said, among other things, 'I am the Immaculate Conception' and 'I do not promise to make you happy in this world but the other'. The story spread like wildfire, Bernadette was canonised in 1933, crutches now hang at the grotto and the little town hosts the most impressive Marian cult in Europe.

ABOVE: 20th-century piety at Lourdes: A statue of St Bernadette in front of an apse mosaic showing the schoolgirl's famous vision of the Virgin Mary.

LEFT: Pilgrims at Lourdes.

Sunday in July, 'Reek Sunday' as it is known, some 60,000 Roman Catholics commemorate Patrick's devotion. It has been described as 'an extraordinary, almost medieval sight. Above you, the line stretches along the brow of Ireland's Holy Mountain till it disappears in the thickening cloud. Below you, hundreds more are on their way up or down. The young are in everything from multi-coloured anoraks and trainers to satin jackets and high heels; the old in tweed jackets and brown boots, like characters from *The Irish RM!*'

At Knock, also in County Mayo, pilgrims visit the site of a vision that was witnessed by the entire village in 1879. St Joseph, the Blessed Virgin Mary and the *Agnus Dei* appeared over the gable of the modest church. In 1979 the villagers persuaded Pope Paul to bless the site on its centenary. On that occasion no fewer than one million Irish men and women, nearly one third of the population of the Republic of Ireland, converged on Knock. Such is the continuing power of miracles, holy places and the spirit of pilgrimage.

It is this enduring spirit which inspires people today, as of old, to set out to walk the ancient ways, visit the holy places and explore the roots of their faith. Whatever the motive for setting out, whatever the hardships encountered along the way, the pilgrim's reward is the secret joy of spiritual discovery.

LEFT: Pilgrims at Knock pay their respects to stones from the simple church where the triple vision appeared in 1879 to the people of this remote village in County Mayo.

✠ Saints & Shrines

Beverley Minster	St John of Beverley
Bromholme, Norfolk	The Holy Rood
Canterbury Cathedral	St Thomas Becket
Chester Cathedral	St Werburgh
Chichester Cathedral	St Richard
Croagh Patrick, County Mayo	St Patrick
Dorchester Abbey, Oxfordshire	St Birinus
Durham Cathedral	St Cuthbert
Ely Cathedral	St Etheldreda
Glastonbury Abbey	St Dunstan
Hailes Abbey, Gloucestershire	The Holy Blood
Hereford Cathedral	St Thomas Cantelupe
Holywell, Flintshire	St Winefrede
Ilam, Staffordshire	St Bertelin
Iona Abbey	St Columba
Knock, County Mayo	St Joseph, Virgin Mary, *Agnus Dei*
Lichfield Cathedral	St Chad (and holy well)
Lincoln Cathedral	St Hugh and Little St Hugh
Lindisfarne Priory	St Cuthbert, Oswald, Aidan
Llandaff Cathedral	St Teilo
Lough Derg, County Donegal	St Patrick
Ripon Cathedral	St Wilfrid
Salisbury Cathedral	St Osmund
St Alban's Cathedral	St Alban
St David's Cathedral	St David (*Dewis*)
St Edmundsbury Cathedral	St Edmund
St Michael's Mount	Archangel Michael
Walsingham, Norfolk	Our Lady
Waltham Abbey, Herts	The Miraculous Cross
Westminster Abbey	Edward the Confessor
Winchester Cathedral	St Swithun
Whitchurch Canonicorum, Dorset	St Candida or Wita
Worcester Cathedral	St Wulfstan
York Minster	St William of York

A T L A N T I C

O C E A N

Iona ✠

Lough Derg ✠

NORTHERN
IRELAND

✠ Knock

✠
Croagh Patrick

EIRE

St Davi

Most of the saints and shrines on the map
are mentioned in this guidebook; however
space does not permit a comprehensive list.